Catherine Dickens:
Outside the Magic Circle

Heera Datta

Catherine Dickens:
Outside the Magic Circle
First published as kindle e book in 2014
Text copyright © 2014 -2018Heera Datta.
isbn-13: 978-1508919643
isbn-10: 150891964X
Also available as eBook
***
Cover Image ©2017-2018Danielle Fiore
Model: Danielle Fiore

*"A man is lucky if he is the
first love of a woman.
A woman is lucky if she is the
last love of a man."*
- Charles Dickens

TABLE OF CONTENTS

Introduction

*O*utside the Magic Circle is part fiction and part fact; less fiction and more fact.

Charles Dickens married Catherine Hogarth on 2nd April, 1836, when he was an upcoming writer and reporter. Soon after marriage, he tasted spectacular success with *The Pickwick Papers*. Other successful serials, *Oliver Twist, Nicholas Nickelby, The Old Curiosity Shop, Barnaby Rudge* followed and in 1846, *Dombey and Son* established him the foremost writer of his time.

Catherine was the daughter of a newspaper editor, and married Charles after a courtship of less than a year. She was the mother of his ten children, his hostess, she accompanied him on his American tour. Charles was an active correspondent and whenever he was away from her, he wrote affectionate letters to her, filled with his news and his concerns about their home and children.

Yet, twenty-one years after they wed, Charles Dickens very publicly separated from her, denouncing her as an unfit mother and wife. He removed her from his home, his life, and the lives of his children. He never saw her again, not even when their son, Walter, died at the age of twenty-three in faraway India.

Many of his friends, who knew the real cause of the separation to be an eighteen-year-old actress, supported Catherine, and paid the price by having Charles turn into an enemy.

Catherine's sister, Georgina, placed her loyalty with her brother-in-law and continued to live with him and the children, while Catherine's other sister, Helen, and the rest of the family, rallied around Catherine.

Charles made the actress, Ellen Ternan, who was as young as his third child, his mistress.

Catherine did not speak against her husband publicly, and did nothing to tarnish his image. However, on her deathbed, she gave her daughter letters that Charles had written to her and said, "Give these to the British Museum, that the world may know he loved me once."

These, then, are the facts. *Outside the Magic Circle* is a fictionalized account of Catherine's life after she was plucked out of her familiar world and thrown to the wolves, as it were, by none other than her husband, the exemplary Charles Dickens, famous for upholding values of home and hearth.

It is told in her voice; sometimes reminiscing, at other times baffled, confused, hurt, angry. It has her tears, her love, and her quest for the meaning of her life, and marriage.

ONE

19th May, 1858

I stand alone in this monstrously huge mansion, Tavistock House. Charles acquired it seven years ago for our large family, and meant it to be our London home for the rest of our lives. Three floors, numerous bedrooms, a schoolroom so large it was converted into a theatre on occasion, the house is now empty except for the servants who are somewhere unseen, my son Charley, my mother, and me.

I've no other option left. Charles is bent upon a separation and will not talk. He has moved out of the house ten days ago. My daughters, Mamie and Kate, young women of twenty and nineteen, and my baby, Edward, just six, whom Charles calls the Noble Plorn, and my sister Georgy, have also left home.

I am told Charles is living in his office and Georgy has taken the girls and Plorn to Gad's Hill, our country home.

Walter, dear boy, is in India, ignorant of what is happening here. My other boys are away at school, all four of them. Yes, I am mother to nine living children but I stand alone in the deep silence of this vast house.

What will happen if I scream? Will the silence shatter? Will I see the fragments, large jagged pieces, splinter into life? What will Charles think if he learns I screamed? No doubt he will disbelieve. He doesn't think I have the capacity to feel anything, definitely not pain.

My mother has come to take me away. She looks defeated. The fight has gone out of her. It has taken Charles only two months to defeat her, and the rest of us.

Helen has not come. She is angry with me. She does not understand why I do not fight for my rights. What rights?

The legal men and Charles' friends have made it clear to me I've no rights. At least not rights that matter. The law will give custody of my minor children to Charles. Except Charley, my firstborn, all my children are minor.

Charles is being ruthless and cruel yet he does not know it. He is convinced he is honorable and generous because he is making me a settlement; it isn't as if he is casting me away penniless. What is honorable about discarding a wife who has borne him children and put up with his wishes? What is generous about separating young children from their mother?

But Charles believes his story and he is capable of getting others believe it too. Is he not the greatest storyteller on both sides of the Atlantic? In the world?

He is clever, he always has been. I've been his wife for twenty- one years and have often seen him drive a hard bargain. He should be happy with this one; it is all to his advantage. He is getting rid of his wife on his terms. I know he will do so in a manner to retain his spotless reputation as a keeper of household virtues.

After waiting for ten days, during which Charles has refused to discuss anything except terms of settlement, I know there is no other course left for me but to go away. I'll go insane if I have to wait any longer in this empty shell of my home.

"Charley," I hesitantly ask my firstborn, "may we first go to Gad's Hill? I want to see Plorn and bless him and the girls. I fear I may not see them again."

Charley flushes in embarrassment and I understand. He does not want to go against his father's wishes. Though Charles has not ordered me, yet, to keep away from the children, both of us know he would not want me at Gad's Hill.

I am surprised and grateful that Charley is standing by me. He is not a minor therefore Charles has no control over him legally but he continues to exert the control built over a lifetime. Charley and the children, my sister Georgy and me, are all accustomed to carrying out

Charles' wishes. His approval and praise are very important to us.

I can't rid myself of the premonition that I will not see my children again. I've been told that the separation will not stop them from coming to me but I know nothing will ever be the same. The children will grow up in a home I will not be permitted to enter, and will soon forget me. They will not know my love, perhaps they will hate me. I should write them notes and tell them they will forever be in my heart but I know I will not do so. Charles has already intimated that the children will do better away from my corrupting influence.

I am no better than Charley. I can't oppose Charles' will.

I tell Charley, "It is better, after all, that we do not go to Gad's Hill. Georgy is there with Plorn. She is good to him."

"Georgy! I'm ashamed to call her my daughter!" my mother says vehemently, "I rue the day I sent her to you and I'm inclined to think Helen and the others are speaking the truth. What has been going on here, Kate? I implore you, tell me the truth so that I can help you and save Georgy from further ruin."

Charley flushes a dark shade of red. He is a young man and would rather not listen to intimate matters pertaining to his parents. I leave him standing in the passage and steer my mother into my room.

"Mama, I don't think matters are that way between them. She holds him in high esteem and he treats her a firm favorite," I say, trying to placate her.

"But you are her sister! Her loyalty is with you, with us. She is a Hogarth, is she not? She has lived with you for sixteen years. She only needed to tell the truth. Her silence is proving Charles' allegations about you true, don't you see? He blames you while he is at fault, chasing after an actress who is young enough to be his daughter. Why doesn't Georgy tell this to his friends and lawyers?"

I've been hearing these arguments for over a month. They lead nowhere. Georgina, my sister, has cast her lot with my husband.

My mother suddenly breaks down. This too is not new. She alternates between anger and tears and only stops when I cry. Then she comforts me.

"Kate, do you realize how difficult this is for me and your father? We have to bear your sorry state and also listen to scandal about Georgy. People are saying terrible things. They say Georgy has lived in sin since she was sixteen. Some gossip even said most of the children are hers which is why she is staying and you are going. And once again there is speculation about Mary."

My mother pauses to wipe her eyes and though I know what she will say, I let her continue.

"Sweet, pure Mary! She must be turning in her grave at the things people say, not that I blame them. I could never understand what Charles calls his great love for

Mary. He wears her ring; he took it off her finger when she breathed her last and instead of giving it to you or us, he swore he would wear it for the rest of his life. He caused quite a scandal when he expressed his wish to be buried in the same grave as her. She was his unmarried sister-in-law and he spoke about joining with her in the other world. Had I not known how sweet and innocent Mary was, I would not have accepted your protestations about your husband's innocence. And now, this? Is the man mad? If there is nothing between him and Georgina and she has this foolish regard for him, he is honour bound to send her away. Let him have his actress and leave you with the children. Why does he have to tear them away? Why is he orphaning them? Why?"

"You haven't been listening to his reasons, Mama. I am not fit to be a wife and mother and the children need their aunt whom they regard as their mother."

My mother dabs her tears away and says, "Don't worry, Kate. We'll keep trying and God willing, you will be back in your home and all this will be but a bad dream. You have decided to leave this house so make haste; it will be less painful that way. Shall I call a maid to help you pack?"

"What should I pack, Mama?" I ask, as helpless as a child who turns to its mother for all the answers.

"Leave the packing. I'll send Helen with Charley later. She will know what to do. Let's go."

My mother leaves the room and I look around me. Like the rest of the house, the room is decorated according to Charles' wishes. Though he had moved out a few months ago, I had not changed anything. The spaces that held his things remain empty, to mock me with the barrenness of my marriage.

I turn back and on an impulse pick up Charles' letters. I know they are filled with the love of a lover and husband and I need to read them again and hold them against my heart.

I leave my home with my head bowed low. I do not look back at the grand imposing façade of the mansion. I fear the servants are all lined up behind the curtains and are watching.

I will never forget this day.

TWO

Sundered

There was no peace for me. Mother, Helen and my other relatives were divided in their opinion about the best way to help me. There was a recent law that allowed a wife to divorce her husband in cases of bigamy, cruelty, or incest.

"Catherine should file a petition. She can site cruelty or even incest. Having relations with a sister-in-law is considered incest," one of my aunts insisted.

"Stop saying that! Georgy is unaccountably foolish but she will not sin in the eyes of God and against her sister!" Mama said.

"How about that actress? He might have married her. Doesn't that amount to bigamy?"

"How do we get the proof? He may have taken her across the channel and set her up in France."

"Will he provide for Kate and the children if she gets a divorce?" an uncle asked.

"Will she get custody if she divorces him, that is the moot question. She will succeed in dragging his name through mud but there is no certainty she will get the children. If she does, how will she support them? Charles has said the children will live with him after the separation but they can visit Catherine. If there is a divorce and he gets custody, he may forbid the children from seeing her," a cousin, who knew a little about the law, argued.

I did not want a divorce; I did not even want a separation. I only wanted my world back wherein I was the wife of a highly respected man of letters and mother to my dear children. But who would serve as my advocate towards a reconciliation?

Our dear friend Mark Lemon was acting for me in matters of settlement. It was Charles' wish that we should not deal directly. He was having Forster speak for him while Mark would look out for my interests.

Mark was unhappy with his role but having accepted it, he was doing his best. Charles was rushing through with the negotiations. He wanted to finish off the business at the earliest. He had set up a frenzy of meetings as soon as I left Tavistock House. I knew he would cite my leaving as proof of my consent for our separation.

"You know how he is," Mark tried to explain, "having seized of an idea, he will not let it go until he realizes it fully. I told Forster we should suspend legalities and let tempers cool but Charles is bent upon this course of action. He refuses to listen and sadly, has been spreading canards about you. It is appalling to see to what ill use he is putting his genius."

Three days later, Charles raised the settlement amount from 400 pounds to 600 pounds per year but extracted a heavy price for it. He made my sister Helen and parents sign a document that read, *"Certain statements have been circulated that such differences are occasioned by circumstances deeply affecting the moral character of Mr. Dickens and compromising the reputation and good name of others, we solemnly declare that we now disbelieve such statements."*

They were also made to promise they would not take any legal action against him.

Charles was convinced Mama and Helen were behind the rumours about his relationships will the actress Ellen Ternan and my sister Georgina. However, they were only repeating what everyone else was speculating, but as they were hurting for me, they were a little more vociferous. Could he not understand?

I signed the document of our separation. It was a long document with a lot of legalities. Had I read it, it is likely I would not have understood half of it but I could not read; tears blurred the piece of paper severing me from my past life, which was a blessed relief.

Helen read the document and was furious. Uncaring of my presence, she read aloud some parts. At some place it was stated that I, Catherine, would not take any legal measures to make him live with or cohabit with me.

"As if you would want to live with that vile creature!" she exclaimed, throwing her arms around me. "You are sweet and kind and gentle! Why would you want to live with that coldhearted man!"

And yet, I wanted nothing more than Charles rushing into the room, tearing the papers, and taking me back home.

THREE

Thrown to the Wolves

My mother's house slowly emptied itself of the guests. The entertainment was over. There were no more arguments, speculations, gossip. What remained was a family that felt like a dog whipped for no reason. All we wanted was to retreat to a corner and lick our wounds.

My father and Charley had the worst of it. My father was a newspaperman and moved in literary circles where everyone was obsessed with Charles Dickens and the great upheaval in his personal life. While Charles met the scandal with righteousness, my father could not do so. The only way Charles could come across as morally clean and spotless was by miring my character. Even though I was not in the wrong, the brush he used to whitewash his reputation, tarred mine.

He did it with a viciousness that left me wondering, "Did I know him at all? Was it really the Charles who laughed and sang and conjured tricks for the children or an evil character out of his own books?"

My father learnt that Charles had written letters during the last months and also told many of our friends that his marriage had been an unhappy one. A mistake, he called it. He told them I was intellectually and in all respects not suited to be his wife.

My mother and Helen wanted me to live with them but I was terrified of displeasing Charles. Charles had conceived a deep hatred for both of them. He had ordered Charley that when the boys visited, on no account were they to speak to their aunt or grandmother. If they did so, they had to be sent back immediately.

I feared Charles might use their presence as a pretext for keeping the boys away from me.

Those were sad days for Charley and me. My heart was breaking but I could not look to my son for comfort because he too was shattered. We suffered the same pain but could not speak of it. If the sorrow had been brought about by a death, if it was a bereavement, we would have shared our grief but now we kept it locked within us and carried it like a heavy burden.

Charles had removed me from my home and life. I was no longer his concern. But he was concerned about Ellen Ternan and Georgina, who was back at Tavistock House filling the role of surrogate mother to my children and loyal friend to Charles. A few weeks after the separation, he printed this public notice in the press:

"*By some means, arising out of wickedness, or out of folly, or out of inconceivable wild chance, or out of all three, this trouble has been the occasion of misrepresentations, mostly grossly false, most monstrous, and most cruel - involving, not only me, but innocent persons dear to my heart... I most solemnly declare, then - and this I do both in my own name and in my wife's name - that all the lately whispered rumours touching the trouble, at which I've glanced, are abominably false. And whosoever repeats one of them after this denial, will lie as willfully and as foully as it is possible for any false witness to lie, before heaven and earth.*"

This was followed by

"*Some domestic trouble of mine, of long-standing, on which I will make no further remark than that it claims to be respected, as being of a sacredly private nature, has lately been brought to an arrangement, which involves no anger or ill-will of any kind, and the whole origin, progress, and surrounding circumstances of which have been, throughout, within the knowledge of my children. It is amicably composed, and its details have now to be forgotten by those concerned in it.*"

He sent me a copy of the statement with a letter stating that he hoped all unkindness was over between us.

"How can he speak for you and make it seem that everything has your consent?" Helen demanded. "Kate, you should also give a statement. Tell everyone the truth about the ornament he sent Ellen."

"Have you forgotten he made you sign a document?" I asked. "My agreement probably bars me from speaking against him but he is free to say whatever he wants. Helen, people listen to what he has to say, editors publish his notices and letters. Can you imagine anyone going against him and publishing my version? Don't forget, I've affixed my signature to the agreement of separation by *mutual consent.*"

I worried about the children. I wanted to see them. I had done everything Charles wanted. I had set him as free as it was possible to do, now all I wanted was the children to come to me.

I asked Charley, "When will the girls and Plorn come? I miss them."

Charley was evasive in his answer but I wouldn't let him be.

"I don't know, Mama. He has forbidden the girls and the older boys from seeing you. Kate told me he is behaving like a mad man, shouting for no reason. Nothing they do is good enough for him."

"He said...I could see the children. Helen tells me it is there in the agreement."

"I spoke to Aunt Georgy. She will make arrangement for Plorn to see you after Father permits."

"Charley, he is so young. He needs his mother. I need him."

18

"I know, I miss them too! How happy we were!" And Charley, my brave son, who at twenty-two was doing something few could even contemplate, he was opposing the great Charles Dickens, broke down and cried like a baby.

I comforted him but my thoughts were with my other children. Did they also weep, and who wiped their tears?

I worried about my sons at school. Charles, in a newspaper statement, had said that the children were aware of what was happening and were content with the changed domestic arrangements. But that was not true. The boys had not known what was coming. Neither had I.

When they had gone to their boarding school at the beginning of the term, there was nothing unusual in their home or between their parents. They must have learnt about the separation, like everybody else, from the newspapers. Their masters, schoolfellows and even the servants would know. Were they objects of pity or cruel jests?

I asked Charley, "Did your father or aunt visit the boys at school?"

"They know what has happened. Father has informed them."

How did Charles inform them, by way of a cold letter or a jolly one saying they were better being rid of their mother? Whatever way he had done it, the children would be cut up. Why did he not understand he was ruining the lives of the children? What about Kate and

Mamie? Would they be received in decent families? They were young women who needed to go into society, to find good husbands. Who would open their doors to them with all this talk about their parents? And even if someone did, how would the girls hold up their heads?

What about Walter, who was in India? The children here could find solace in one another but Walter was alone. Charles had sent him to the colonies last year, at a time when we were hearing dreadful stories about the Sepoy Mutiny. Walter was only sixteen and did not want to go but had bowed to his father's strong will and had tearfully set off on the long voyage. He was now a soldier in India, living in a harsh climate that was ill-suited to his health. News from England reached India quickly. He must know his world back home was irrevocably changed. What would he have made of Charles' statements to the press?

My parents and my sister often visited me, as did a few other relatives. I tried not to break down in their presence and kept my anger and my heartbreak for the privacy of my bedroom. Whatever tears I shed, I shed them alone and such tears are bitter and cold; they only freeze the pain but do not lessen it.

I was filled with desperation to see Plorn and the girls. I tried to think of ways to catch a glimpse of them. Maybe I could don a bonnet with a long veil, wrap myself in a voluminous shawl and spy on them? But I lacked the courage. For the last twenty-two years Charles had emphatically taken all decisions pertaining to me so though my heart yearned for my children, I could not decide how to set up a meeting. Neither could I challenge Charles.

My father had been Charles' sponsor when he was yet to make his mark. He had introduced Charles to our household. Naturally, he was now upset with the way things had turned out but was able to contain his anger much better than my mother.

Two months after my separation, he told me, "Charles was confident he could bluster out of this mess. Instead of retreating from society like a gentleman would, he has been giving readings to packed audiences. As he is always a great success with the public, he must have thought that his public appearances and his personal notices in the press would absolve him of all blame. He would have hoped he could continue as before."

"Is that not happening?" I asked. "I do not read of any public outcry. He still continues to be the Keeper of English Morality."

"The public has swallowed his version but you have a number of champions among his friends. They believe he has treated you very shabbily. They would even call on you to show you support but.."

"No, please, I could not bear that. Not at the moment, at least."

"I understand. I hope Charles sees the error of his ways. Apart from Forster who is his loyal friend, the only people I see with him are those who are not very respectable and lead questionable lives, like William Macready and Wilkie Collins. He is no longer friendly with Thackeray. He cannot have failed to notice the lack of warmth in his reception by reputable people."

My father's words gave me some hope but it was cruelly dashed a few days later. The New York Tribune published another of Charles' statements and the press in England reprinted it. This statement was shocking in its deceit and cruelty.

In the open letter, Charles stated that our marriage had been unhappy for many years and that Georgina Hogarth, his sister-in-law, was responsible for long preventing a separation by her care for the children: *"She has remonstrated, reasoned, suffered and toiled, again and again to prevent a separation between Mrs. Dickens and me."*

He blamed me for the separation. Not only blamed but made it sound as if by separating from me he was fulfilling my heart's desire. *"Her always increasing estrangement made a mental disorder under which she sometimes labours - more, that she felt herself unfit for the life she had to lead as my wife and that she would be better far away."*

What was this mental disorder and if he was the solicitous husband he claimed to be, why had no doctor treated me for it?

Cruel, cruel, Charles. He played the martyr and boasted of his financial generosity to me. Without spelling it out, his statements proclaimed, 'Look at me! I was tied to a woman who is little better than a lunatic. I suffered silently and bore as much as I could until, for the sake of my innocent children, it became necessary to remove her from our home. Behold my generosity! I did not leave her penniless. No sir! She has a comfortable income. Lucky woman! Poor me!'

He was a writer, wasn't he, and he knew how to set a plot and assign roles. Having cast me as a mentally disordered wife, he needed someone as caretaker for which he chose Georgina and praised her as having *a higher claim on his affection, respect and gratitude than anybody in the world.*

My family rallied around me as did a few friends. Of course, none of us knew what we were to do about these falsehoods.

Georgina added her voice to his and told whoever would listen that *"By some constitutional misfortune and incapacity, my sister always from their infancy, threw her children upon other people, consequently as they grew up, there was not the usual strong tie between them and her - in short, for many years, although we have put a good face upon it, we have been very miserable at home."*

These were her exact words in her letter to Maria Winter and they soon got around.

"Georgina is parroting Charles!" my mother's friend, who had seen the letter, told us. She sounded most surprised.

What surprised me was that Georgina had written to Maria Beadnell Winter at all, and that too as if to an intimate friend. I knew Georgy did not like her. She thought her gossipy and insincere. Is that why she had written? Was this the equivalent of Charles' letters in the newspapers?

I asked Charley, "You do believe I've no mental disorder, don't you, Charley?"

He dashed away a tear and held me in his embrace.

"Charley, what is wrong with your father? Why is he behaving like this?"

"I don't know. Katey says he is behaving like a mad man. He does not rest, and is away most of the time. He is presently on a provincial tour."

"Charley, my reputation is in tatters. No doubt everyone will run and hide when they see me next or even send me to Bedlam. But I worry about the children. Will the boys not suffer at school? How about you, Charley? How do you face your friends?"

"It's not so bad," he said bravely.

Both of us did not allude to the part of the letter that spoke about Ellen Ternan.

"Two wicked persons who should have spoken very differently of me... have... coupled with this separation the name of a young lady for whom I've a great

24

attachment and regard. I will not repeat her name - I honour it too much. Upon my soul and honour, there is not on this earth a more virtuous and spotless creature than this young lady. I know her to be as innocent and pure, and as good as my own dear daughters."

I knew very well that the separation for which Charles laid the blame at my door had much to do with Ellen. I wondered what I would have done had he set her up discreetly as his mistress, like it was whispered about so many other writers we knew.

Would I have objected and tried to divorce him or, like other wives, turned a blind eye and immersed myself in my home and children? If the price was leaving my children, I very much think I would have done the latter.

FOUR

The Unkindest Cut

I had my wish at last. Georgina made arrangements for the boys to see me. I was delighted to have them with me and I could see their happiness in being with their Mama.

The boys had been prepared so they did not ask questions except for Plorn who wanted to know when I would return 'home'.

The visit went on very well but I could sense the boys were getting a little restless indoors, in the cramped quarters. I decided to take them out. As I could not take them to my mother's because of Charles' ban, I took them to visit with Miss Coutts.

Miss Coutts had long been a close friend of Charles. She took his advice even about personal matters and he helped her in her charitable works, especially in running a home for unfortunate women. I knew Miss Coutts to be a woman of noble character. Though she was more

Charles' friend than mine, she had called upon me after the separation and sincerely commiserated with me on my troubles. She had even tried to reason with Charles before he took the extreme step of a public separation.

I took the boys to see Miss Coutts and she was delighted with them. She watched with sympathy the way my younger ones clung to me, as if they already feared a separation.

When we were at the end of the visit, she pressed my hand and murmured, "It pains my heart to see your affliction." She spoke these words of sympathy with such sweetness and sincerity that I was much distressed. I had been alone and lonely and had ceased to expect sympathy from anyone outside my family. I thought everyone viewed me as a confused, crazy woman.

"I'll do what I can, my dear, and try to reason with that stubborn husband of yours," she promised.

Charles was still touring Scotland and Ireland. Miss Coutts wrote him a letter about my visit with the children. I visited her again on some pretext but my real reason was to know whether she had succeeded in softening Charles' stance.

The poor woman, with great reluctance, showed me Charles' letter to her. He had attacked me mercilessly. He said,

... since we spoke of her before, she has caused me unspeakable agony of mind; and I must plainly put before you what I know to be true ... She does not – and

she never did – care for the children: and the children do not – and they never did – care for her. The little play that is acted in your Drawing-room is not the truth, and the less the children play it, the better for themselves ... O Miss Coutts do I not know that the weak hand that never could help or serve my name in the least, has struck at it – in conjunction with the wickedest people, whom I've loaded with benefits! I want to communicate with her no more. I want to forgive and forget her ... From Walter away in India, to little Plornish at Gad's Hill there is a grim knowledge among them ... that what I now write, is the plain bare fact. She has always disconcerted them; they have always disconcerted her; and she is glad to be rid of them, and they are glad to be rid of her.

She is glad to be rid of them, and they are glad to be rid of her: the words echoed in my mind for a long, long time. They brought fresh tears whenever I remembered them. My arms ached to hold my children, my ears longed to hear them call out to me, and my heart bled for them and yet, Charles said I was glad to be rid of them. Did he teach the children the same untruths, so that they would come to hate me?

Later that year, I moved to a house in Gloucester Crescent, near Regent's Park, the house purchased for me according to the terms of separation from Charles. The house and 600 pounds a year, I would be respectably placed for the rest of my life. *Of the pecuniary part of them I will only say that I believe they are as generous*

28

as if Mrs. Dickens were a lady of distinction, and I a man of fortune. Charles had published this too. Such a kind and generous husband!

Moving into the house was a painful experience. There was none of the expectant joy associated with my earlier changes of address. There was no hustle and bustle; no Charles to energetically rush about and supervise the placement of every single piece of furniture and ornament.

It was a sad moving, like moving into a tomb or coffin. It was actually worse than that because here I mourned my own self.

By now I feared my circumstances would not change. I would be a wife in name only, a wife only because my husband could not find a reason to divorce me. He had made his case and rested it in front of the world and I am sure there were many who pitied him for his condition and wished me dead so that their beloved Charles Dickens could marry again and be happy.

Only one thing lifted my spirits when I moved into the house. Either by accident or design, the house was situated opposite the one where Mamie and Kate took music lessons.

I did not know on which days the girls would come for their lessons. I spent the first two days sitting by the window, my eyes glued on the road, with the curtain discreetly drawn except for a tiny crack to view the road. I even took my meals there.

My daughters came on the third day. They left the carriage and hurried into the house opposite mine.

They were perhaps late for their lessons, I thought, and continued to wait. When they came out, I drew the curtain aside but they hurried into the carriage with bowed heads.

"Charley," I asked him as soon as he came in, "did you not tell Kate and Mamie that I reside here?"

"I did. Why?"

"Nothing. I just wondered."

And thus I stood behind the curtain and watched them come and go into the house opposite mine. I am sure they were aware of my regard because they did not speak to each other or look around. Instead, they hurried into the waiting carriage with set expressions: Mamie looking defiant and Kate ashamed.

Charley caught me watching one day. "Mother, it is difficult for them," he explained, "you don't know how it is with them. Father does not want them to have any contact with you. He gets angry if you are mentioned and though he tells them he will not stop them from coming to you, he does not encourage them to do so. They are confused and unhappy."

"As are you, dear boy," I said, patting him lightly on the cheek.

But Kate was made of sterner stuff and one day she walked right in. I was, as usual, at the window. The carriage stopped. Kate got down. She was alone. Instead

30

of going for her lesson, she looked up at the window telling me what I already knew: she had been aware of my unseen presence all this time.

She knocked at my door and when the maid opened it, she rushed into my arms.

It was as if the intervening months of separation had never been. What is it about daughters that we can open the floodgates of our heart? What I had yearned to do all these months, I did now. I wept like I had never before. I wept and Kate kept wiping my tears. "Stop, Mama please," she said again and again.

"Where is Mamie? Will she come next time?"

"Mamie has a bad cold and she has not come today. She has changed, Mama. She does exactly what Aunt Georgy tells her. She doesn't even speak to me about you. I only came to beg your forgiveness for not coming to see you but I couldn't, for Mamie would tell!"

"I understand, child."

"You must be thinking us all wicked but it's not our fault. It's his and I hate him!"

Now it was Kate's turn to cry and mine to comfort. Kate secretly visited me twice more before she was found out. The driver must have told. Charley told me Charles was punishing Kate for her transgression by ignoring her.

My life slowly settled into a pattern of endless waiting and hoping.

FIVE

Barren

More than once Charles had grumbled I was too fertile. Charley was born just nine months after our marriage. Between Charley and Plorn there are sixteen years. During these sixteen years, I gave birth ten times and miscarried three times.

And yet I now led a barren life. My sister Georgy, spinster aunt, has been lauded in her role as mother to my children.

My days stretch endlessly. There are no meals to plan, no servants to supervise. I know how to mix a Twelfth Night cake large enough to feed thirty people with ease; I know just the right type of oysters to tickle my husband's palate; I can sew and embroider and act as hostess.

The sad truth is I need these skills no longer. I am not inclined to plan meals; I eat whatever the maid prepares, so does Charley. I've no interest in the house. I've stopped plying my needle because there is nothing to mend, and what pretty things can a desolate heart create?

Charles was right. I've a mental disorder. I do not have the ability to think. Instead of feeling sorry for myself, I should have gone about the separation in a clearheaded manner, the way he had done. The law gave Charles the custody but I should have insisted on the children spending time with me. Instead I believed Charles when he said, 'Nobody is taking away your children. They will be in the care of their aunt and me, that is all."

What would I not give to kiss away one of Plorn's little cuts and mend the tears in his clothes!

Some old friends visit me but there is awkwardness on my part and on theirs. Helen comes often and tries to engage me with music. Music runs in our family.

I do not want to spend much time with old friends and I don't know how to make new friends. Even if I find the courage to do so, everyone knows my personal history. Who will want to consort with a woman known for not caring for her children? Even I would not, in my earlier life, and that is why I find it so difficult to live with myself.

One day I took the maid and went into the park. I found myself a secluded bench and watched the children playing. Most of them were with their governesses but there were a few young mothers too.

A woman sat beside me. She was about my age and by her dress, looked to be a widow. We might not have spoken except that a young child running close to the bench stumbled and fell. We both helped the child.

The woman was pleasant- faced and spoke like a gentlewoman. She shared anecdotes about her grandchildren, two of them being of the same age as the child we had helped.

She liked to talk and I passed a very pleasant hour. For the first time in months, I didn't feel like I was being observed. Though the friends who called were invariably kind and tactful, I knew they wondered about my emotions. They were curious as to how I had adapted to my solitary existence; they wondered whether I had heard about Charles and his actress. And I feared they wondered about the kind of mother I was.

That hour was a blessed relief. I was free of the constraint of being discarded wife and mother. I was someone faceless in whom nobody had a vestige of vulgar curiosity.

The woman, who was a Mrs. Evans from the country, come to visit her married daughter, looked at me searchingly and asked, "Forgive me, my dear, have you suffered a bereavement?"

I nodded.

"Your husband."

When I again nodded, she said, "You poor dear, I could tell by your face. You are not bearing up well, I fear. I know it is a difficult cross to bear, I lost my dear sainted John two years ago, but I've learnt to find comfort in my children and grandchildren. You should try that dear. Do you have children?"

When I did not answer, she continued, "Ah, that makes it difficult. My sister is a widow and finds the going very difficult because her marriage was barren."

I did not correct her about me being the mother of nine living children. At that moment, the children I had carried in sickness and brought forth in pain and hardship seemed like phantom children. They had been born but had drifted away like wraiths.

Only little Dora seemed real. Beautiful, delightful Dora, whom the merciful lord had taken away when she was only eight months old. I had not understood then but I realized now it was a good thing my daughter had died an infant. She would have been twelve now. Being a girl, she would not have the escape of school and would have remained in misery in a divided household. Dear beloved Dora was happier in a better world.

I said, "My marriage was not barren. I had a daughter but she died an infant."

Mrs. Evans dabbed at her eyes and recalled her two infants she had buried.

That night I realized a sorry truth. From now onwards I would have nothing to say to women except about the death of a child. The usual conversation of husband and children and household matters was forever closed to me.

SIX

Early Days

I spent a lot of time in bed. I was perpetually tired. Helen chided me and said I would feel better if I exerted myself but I could not shake off my low spirits.

I often remembered the days before my marriage. My father was a wonderful man. He was a scholar of music and a writer and more important, he was bighearted. There was nothing petty about him. My father knew Walter Scott and Lockhart well, and my grandfather, my mother's father, had been on the friendliest of terms with Robert Burns.

Though we were a cultured family and had close links with literary persons of importance, my parents were not snobbish. They shared their recollections of these men of letters. We read their books and other books too. It is difficult to say what was more important, books or music, because both filled our home. My father had immense knowledge about music and encouraged us to play for the joy of it.

When I was nineteen, my father brought Charles, my future husband, home. My father was then the co-editor of the Chronicle, to which Charles contributed sketches under the name of Boz.

My father found his gifted and as was his practice, took him to heart. At first, me and my sister Mary did not know what to make of Charles. He was quite unlike anyone we knew.

Mary was then fifteen, four years younger to me, but we were very close and shared our views about clothes and fashions and young men. I suspect we were quite as foolish as any other young lady in those pursuits and as happy too.

Charles was a young man of twenty-two but quite dashing in embroidered silk overcoats and fancy neck cloths. He talked and laughed a lot and at times even acted out parts from a play. He was totally unaffected and livened up our gatherings. At first I thought him to be playing the dandy but after meeting him a few more times I found his conversation quite improving. Father was right; Charles was talented and had a good future.

My sister and cousins teased me that Charles favored me over everyone else with his attentions and I knew this to be true. There was nothing shrinking or bashful about Charles and soon we had an understanding. We went for long walks or spent time together seated in the plentiful gardens and orchards around the house.

I came to love Charles quite foolishly. I found him handsome and charming. He had compelling eyes. I remember asking Mary, "What do you think he sees in me? Tell me how I look. Look at me as a young man would and not as a sister."

So Mary stood me in the centre and slowly walked around me with the affected walk of a young tulip. She looked so funny we soon fell into each other's arms, giggling.

But of course I knew Charles found me quite lovely. He often told me he loved the way I looked. He loved my blue eyes, which he said were quite mysterious, my golden hair and the ringlets that framed my face, and my form which was slim yet right enough to be an armful.

We spoke many foolish, pretty things like young lovers everywhere do. He swore I was the prettiest, gentlest of creatures while I protested he was merely flattering me.

I said, "I know of many young women who are prettier than I. I can point them out to you. Some of them veritably sparkle like diamonds."

He turned serious and held my hand to his heart. "That may be but they are also cold and hard and brittle while you are kind and gentle. I look forward to have you as my sweet wife sitting by the fireside while I toil over my stories."

Charles took rooms in Selwood Terrace which was close to my home. He wanted to be closer to his love, he privately confided to me.

He was forever writing sweet, ardent letters, sending his love and a million kisses, and making me laugh with his foolish love names. I was his 'Dear Mouse', his 'Darling Tatie', his very own 'Dearest Darling Pig.'

Some of my relatives thought I could do better because Charles was not a man of means. I would be leaving my home for his rented rooms, which were suitable for a bachelor home. But I did not mind. I loved him and was happy he loved me in turn, so it did not matter where we lived.

We also spent a lot of time apart because Charles was very busy working as a reporter for the newspaper, following political events and also reviewing plays. He travelled to different places and wrote late into the night. But our love did not wane. Charles made time to write to me frequently. His career was looking up. His work was being appreciated. He was fortunate to meet people who wanted to publish his stories and sketches in the form of a book. He also secured work writing a monthly episode for a newspaper, which would pay 14 pounds per episode. The amount would be enough for us to set up house.

We were married a year later, on 2nd of April, 1836, in a simple ceremony at St.Luke's church in Chelsea. Charles gifted me a workbox, inscribed 'From Charles

Dickens to Kate'. He also went to great pains to purchase furniture for our new home.

Our honeymoon was spent in Chalk, a pretty village on the marshes of North Kent. Charles was already working on the Pickwick Papers then and we laughed together over the drafts.

After our honeymoon, we moved into rooms at Furnival's Inn. Charles had furnished the suite of rooms with new furniture, rosewood for the drawing room, mahogany for the dining room; the sideboard, decanters, jugs, china jars were all new, and I was eager to prove myself an excellent household manager.

While Charles spent his time at the newspaper office or out reporting, I busied myself in the little house, trying to decorate it the way I wanted. This proved a little difficult because Charles had *his* ideas about how our home should look.

"This is for me to do Charles," I scolded.

"Yes, dear heart, but you are sadly inexperienced."

"I am not. I am twenty and you may ask Mama, fully able to take care of a much larger household. She has trained me, Charles, and I've been helping with the house and the children."

"That is different. You are experienced in the ways of your father, now you have a husband to please."

"My father never comes in the way of my mother. She takes care of the housekeeping and the children, while he has his own work."

40

"That may be now. Perhaps he guided her in the early days of their marriage until they were both of one mind."

I could never answer his arguments, which he followed with sweet words of love. I soon learnt that Charles was never happy unless things were done exactly the way he liked.

I did mind a little but I could never abide a quarrel and I liked to see Charles cheerful. He could be an entertaining companion.

Another reason I accepted his behavior, and one that would have surprised him, was my knowledge about his insecurity. He had lived a difficult life until then, and to him the idea of a home was very dear. It was an ideal he grew up with, a picture he had painted in his innermost recesses.

When he married me, it was not as other young men do, with only a casual notion about married life. Charles saw his life, his home clearly; he saw me by the fireside, and him at the desk, working on his stories. He saw his dream coming true. He saw every picture he had dreamt of taking shape. That was why he himself furnished our home, and arranged it exactly the way he wanted, or rather, had imagined. I knew this in my love for him, and allowed him his happiness.

My dear Mary was naturally eager to see how I fared as housekeeper and wife, and she visited us often. Charles welcomed her presence and enjoyed listening to her. He told me she was like sunshine and indeed, my dear sister was all that was pleasing.

I was pregnant within a month of my marriage. I was sick frequently but Mama assured me it was normal. I knew it was a woman's lot and tried to bear the discomfort. My mother and the landlady sent delicacies to tempt me. Mary visited quite often and cheered me with her conversation. She was the best of sisters.

Charles was very busy. *Pickwick Papers* was very well received and this brought publishers to him. He was able to make arrangements with four different publishers, for books he promised to write. We were both delighted with his success.

Charles decided he needed a break from newspaper work; he took leave of absence for five weeks, during which he took me to the village of Petersham in Surrey, between Richmond Park and the Thames.

I was halfway through my pregnancy and the sickness had subsided. Charles said I was glowing with impending motherhood. I felt deeply contented and loved the feel of my baby growing in me. We stayed at an inn and enjoyed the scenic walks. Charles was careful of my condition and did not keep his usual brisk pace.

SEVEN

He Giveth and He Taketh

*P*ickwick Papers continued to do well. Charles got more writing offers. He had to resign from his job as reporter from the paper.

The midwife was satisfied with my progress but Mama was anxious because it was my first confinement. By the last month of my pregnancy, I was lying down in bed all the time. My feet were swollen and my back ached.

When I went into labour, Mama and Charles' mother were with me. Mary also had come but as she was unmarried, she was shooed away from my side.

As I lurched between one pain and the next, the mothers talked about their birthings. They had a score of midwives tales to compare.

Charles did not stay at home. He took Mary with him, to look for a table for my room.

Mama laughed. "Your young man is not brave enough to hear you crying out!"

My mother-in-law laughed too. "None of them are. They cry at the smallest scratch and moan when they are down with something as small as a head cold. It is we women who are strong enough to undergo this pain again and again."

Charley was born in the evening, on the festival of Twelfth Night.

The birth had been difficult but I was delighted to hold my very own baby in my arms. I was a mother, which was a blessed thing. But for some reason I was not able to nurse the child. I tried again and again and wept when little Charley shrieked with hunger, his whole body red with the effort.

A wet nurse was found for Charley. Mama consoled me that it was not an uncommon occurrence. Many women had problem nursing, it was not a worrying matter; children grew up the same way whoever nursed them. What was important was I did not suffer from fever, which sometimes set in after childbirth.

I should have been a happy young mother but I was miserable. I had no appetite and I felt tearful all the time. What kind of mother was I that I could not feed my child?

My mother grew worried over my continued despondency. She knew some women went insane after giving birth.

Charles tried his best to lift my spirits. He even tried feeding me when I refused food. But he was extremely busy with his work and I spent many lonely hours utterly dejected. It is only in recent years I've come to understand from a matron that my condition was not an uncommon one. Depression sometimes sets in after childbirth. The confinement aggravates, and even causes it. Being isolated, away from fresh air and exercise, leads to low spirits.

But I did not know it then and often found myself engulfed in the blackest of despair. Charles decided a change of scene would do all of us good and took us to Chalk, the same place we had our honeymoon.

Mary, the baby, and his nurse came with us and the trip helped me. Charles was of course busy writing, though he also got much needed fresh air and exercise. I soon lost my despondency of the last two months and started taking care of my baby boy and even enjoying my husband's attentions.

Charles was doing very well, there was more money, and we moved from Furnival's to a fine house in Doughty street. It was a large house at a good address on a pleasant shady street.

Mary continued to live with us, and had her own bedroom. We were happy in the new house. Charles was very fond of Mary, actually everyone who met her was struck by her delicate beauty and pleasing manners.

But a terrible sorrow was soon to befall us. Two months after we moved into the house, Mary suddenly died. She was just seventeen.

She had accompanied Charles and me to the theatre and took ill after we returned home. She cried out loudly and Charles rushed to her room. He found her prostrate, still in her day clothes. We called the doctor in and sent for my mother.

The doctor could do nothing for Mary. Though she breathed, she was insensible for fourteen hours. Charles tried to revive her with brandy. He raised her in his arms and tried to spoon the brandy but very soon after that, she died, still held gently by Charles. Her eyes fluttered open for a moment, she saw his face and murmured his name and then she was gone.

Mary's death was a great shock to all of us. She had been a healthy young woman on Saturday and was no more on Sunday. My mother was inconsolable, weeping and even losing consciousness. Charles' grief was no less alarming. I had to put aside my grief and become strong for my mother and for my husband. But I did not remain unscathed. I miscarried.

Charles made all arrangements for the funeral. He decided the place of burial and the words to go on the tombstone. *"Mary Scott Hogarth. Died 7th May 1837. Young, Beautiful and Good, God in His Mercy Numbered Her With His Angels at the Early Age of Seventeen"*.

My mother was not very happy with him taking charge but I convinced her that Mary was as dear to Charles as his sister Fanny was. Moreover her death in our house had shocked him deeply.

However, during the coming months and years there would be many times when I fervently hated Mary, and repented too for this hatred, because Mary could not have known what her death would do to Charles. She genuinely loved Charles with the innocent and pure love of a sister.

However, my mother, aunts, and even I were forced to question Charles's feelings. None of us asked him directly but his behavior embarrassed them and pained me.

Charles had removed Mary's ring before she was prepared for the funeral and he now wore it. He said the ring would never be off his finger as long as he lived. He did not let me send Mary's clothes to my mother. He packed them away himself, caressing them gently while tears coursed down his cheeks.

"What do you want to do with them?" I asked.

He just shook his head and pressed his face in the gown he was holding, inhaling deeply. I stood beside him and stared. I was deeply shocked by Mary's death but Charles looked shattered, as if his life spring was broken.

He let out an anguished sigh. "I miss her so much, Kate," he said. I wish we could go back in time, we could go to Furnivel's, we were all so happy there, I feel we will find her happy spirit brightening those rooms."

"Charles, Mama wants Mary's things. Mary was her daughter whom she has lost suddenly. It will console her to have Mary's clothes and ring."

"No," Charles said firmly, "she has Mary's other things. But I've only these to remember my angel. And she was an angel, a sweet angel come to brighten our home and hearth, wasn't she, Kate?"

Charles packed away all of Mary's things and put them away, I don't know where. "They are in a secret place, let them moulder away," he told me. He also had a lock of Mary's hair and he kept it in a box on his table.

A few months later my mother took me aside. She looked troubled. "What exactly was Mary to Charles?" she asked bluntly.

"Why Mama... she was his dear sister."

"I don't want to sully the memory of my sweet daughter but was there any....she was young and innocent...was there any...did Charles....was there any impropriety in their behavior?"

"No Mama. How could there be? I lived there too."

"You were unwell a lot of times, more so in the weeks after the baby. You wanted to be left alone. I would have brought Mary back but I thought she would cheer you up."

"Why are you asking me all this?"

"Because your husband is causing talk, that is why! He met one of your uncles and spent an hour talking about Mary. He showed him Mary's ring and said it was the dearest thing to him on earth. He said he wanted to be buried with Mary, he wanted to join her in the life after."

"I'll speak to him," I said but knew I would not. Mary had become an obsession with him and nobody knew it better than me.

He dreamt about Mary and mumbled her name in his sleep. He compared everything I did with Mary. If we went out, he tried to go to the places we had visited with Mary and recalled every minute of it, even her clothes. But there was something infinitely worse that he did: in the most intimate moments between us as husband and wife, he sometimes sighed and I knew he was thinking about Mary.

Charles has wronged me in many ways. He has taken away my home and my children. But I rank equally high the wrong he has done in making me sometimes hate my dear sainted sister, and staining her good name. For people have long memories. When he separated from me and praised Georgina, many older relatives whispered that Charles had succeeded in seducing two of George Hogarth's girls.

EIGHT

Happy Days

A month after my miscarriage I was again pregnant. I kept house with the help of a cook and a maid, and tried to do it exactly the way Charles wanted. He was a tyrant in certain things, though he did not mean to. It was just that he wanted the house in a certain way and he wouldn't allow me to do things my way. I was never stubborn so I tried to follow his instructions in all matters pertaining to the house and my person. He even liked to go over the menu of the next meal but he made a game out of it many times.

I recollected the pleasure with which I had set about making a home, the joy of trying out new recipes, and the dismay of having it all criticized by my husband. I would try out a dish or an arrangement, and show it with housewifely importance to Mary, who was always suitably impressed. "You are a capital housekeeper, Kate," she would tell me. But Charles would find some flaw, and argue until I agreed that indeed, what I had done could be improved upon. *Only then* he would praise me, and express the hope I would better my efforts in future.

The admonishments and ill humor, and mockery, all cleverly couched in pleasant words, gradually chipped away at my confidence, and I did not realize it. It was only later when I was evicted out, it was an eviction though Charles called it a separation by mutual consent, I found how much of myself I had lost in my years with Charles. Alone, I had difficulty in deciding even small matters. Charles had made me so dependant that I could not fight him effectively when he turned me out. It was the same story as before. He decided and then insisted it was want I wanted and it was good for me and our family.

A friend of my mother told me, after Charles published a note about our 'unhappy' marriage in the newspaper, that strong-willed men need wives who will not buckle down.

I do not know if that is true. I like to believe that by giving in to Charles' whims, I gave him the freedom to write. I wonder how things would have been if I had quarreled with him over the purchase of every knife and fork. Yes, Charles saw to those too.

Mary's death shattered both of us but I had to be the stronger of the two because Charles would just not make the effort. He even stopped writing and naturally was not able to send the episodes of *Pickwick Papers* and *Oliver Twist*. His grief was frightening in the extreme.

But he came out of the abyss. Forster was a big help, and our life slowly resumed its normalcy. I was careful not to mention Mary to him and whenever he spoke of her, I tried to dwell on her kindness and how it would pain her to see him suffering.

My pregnancy went the way of my first, except that I knew what to expect. There was no Mary to help me while away the tedious hours, nor Mama to give me frequent advice. But there was baby Charley and he was my joy and comfort.

I've never confessed it to anyone nor shall I but I wept many private tears during those days. I was increasing with our child but Charles, when he was not working, had thoughts only of Mary. One night, when I was unable to sleep, I left our bed and went into Charles' study, for a book. His diary was on the table. I could not stop myself from opening it. Later I wished I had not because those entries festered in my mind and left me depressed even after childbirth.

Monday, January 1st, 1838.

A sad New Year's Day in one respect, for at the opening of last year poor Mary was with us. Very many things to be grateful for since then, however. Increased reputation and means—good health and prospects. We never know the full value of blessings till we lose them (we were not ignorant of this one when we had it, I hope). But if she were with us now, the same winning, happy, amiable companion, sympathising with all my thoughts and feelings more than anyone I knew ever did or will, I think I should have nothing to wish for, but a continuance of such happiness. But she is gone, and pray God I may one day, through his mercy, rejoin her.

Saturday, January 6th, 1838.

Our boy's birthday—one year old. A few people at night—only Forster, the De Gex's, John Ross, Mitton, and the Beards, besides our families—to twelfth-cake and forfeits.

This day last year, Mary and I wandered up and down Holborn and the streets about for hours, looking after a little table for Kate's bedroom, which we bought at last at the very first broker's which we had looked into, and which we had passed half-a-dozen times because I didn't like to ask the price. I took her out to Brompton at night, as we had no place for her to sleep in (the two mothers being with us); she came back again next day to keep house for me, and stopped nearly the rest of the month. I shall never be so happy again as in those chambers three storeys high—never if I roll in wealth and fame. I would hire them to keep empty, if I could afford it.

Sunday, January 14th, 1838.

To church in the morning, and when I came home I wrote the preceding portion of this diary, which henceforth I make a steadfast resolution not to neglect, or paint.[11] I've not done it yet, nor will I; but say what rises to my lips—my mental lips at least—without reserve. *No other eyes will see it, while mine are open in life, and although I daresay I shall be ashamed of a good deal in it, I should like to look over it at the year's end.*

In Scott's diary, which I've been looking at this morning, there are thoughts which have been mine by day and by night, in good spirits and bad, since Mary died.

"Another day, and a bright one to the external world again opens on us; the air soft, and the flowers smiling, and the leaves glittering. They can't refresh her to whom mild weather was a natural enjoyment. Cerements of lead and of wood already hold her; cold earth must have her soon. But it is not . . . . (she) who will be laid among the ruins. . . . . She is sentient and conscious of my emotions somewhere—where, we can't tell, how, we can't tell; yet would I not at this moment renounce the mysterious yet certain hope that I shall see her in a better world, for all that this world can give me.

"I've seen her. There is the same symmetry of form, though those limbs are rigid which were once so gracefully elastic; but that yellow masque with pinched features, which seems to mock life rather than emulate it, can it be the face that was once so full of lively expression? I will not look upon it again."

I know but too well how true all this is.

The words were no different from what Charles spoke during the day. They were the same that I read in his face when he became silent in my company. But seeing them in his diary chilled me and made me feel terribly alone, especially as there was no mention of me anywhere. He remembered the day spent with Mary but had forgotten that I spent the very same day in labour.

I sat alone in the dark for a long time. When I went back to bed, Charles was murmuring Mary's name. I shook him awake rather roughly.

I kept myself aloof from Charles. I was just not up to listening about Mary, though I missed her terribly and would have liked to speak about her with anybody else. Sometimes he noticed my silence and tried to talk to me. He spoke about his new friends and the theatre and his writing. I responded as best as I could but he sensed a difference in me. He confided in Forster that he feared we were not compatible.

I went into confinement and three weeks later a daughter was born on 6th March, just ten months after Mary's death. Naturally, we christened her Mary, though we called her Mamie.

I was again ill after the birth. Charles thought it was the same affliction I had after Charley's birth but the truth was I felt very unloved and alone and this was what lay behind my depression.

Kate arrived the following October, after a long labour lasting twelve hours. After her birth we moved to a bigger house, No 1, Devonshire Terrace.

Walter arrived next, after a miscarriage. Charles and I were not even five years into our marriage and we had four little ones.

It was not that Charles was a tyrant all the time or he was morose. There was no one who even came close enough in his jocularity. He could unaided keep us all in splits. He loved the children and made much of them. He named all of them himself and brushed aside my suggestions. To him the naming of our children had become a way of honoring his dear friends.

Other than Charley and Mamie, the rest of our children had embedded in their names the names of writers and artists. Each child embodied a dream for Charles. He saw them all as having the spark of genius, yet he gave them absurd pet names.

I loved Charles with all my heart and I was proud to be his wife. He was happy by how I conducted myself. As his circle of friends grew, he often invited them home and when we were on a holiday, he liked nothing better than to invite them down to the country. "They like you," he told me, "they compliment me on my pretty wife with her natural manners."

Sometimes he was bewildered, as was I, with the rapidity of our increasing family. He was twenty-nine and I was twenty-six and we were already responsible for four little lives.

"Some women don't have so many children," he once grumbled, when I was attending to Mamie who was incessantly crying, and Charles wanted me to listen to his reading.

I was tired and harried and naturally got annoyed. What had he to complain of? It was I who dealt with the nausea and the aches and the terrible pain, and also the debilitating miscarriages. "You make it sound as if I've had all these children by myself."

"I didn't say that."

"You did and I did not know you were not happy with the children."

"I love them and you know that but the children have changed you. You are no longer appreciative of my thoughts and.. my writing. I sometimes wonder whether we are even well suited."

This was too much. Naturally, we quarreled and also made up in the usual way, luckily for Charles not starting another baby.

The children were my joy and I prided myself in being a good mother. I also loved cooking and knew all of Charles' favourite dishes. He loved good food and liked inviting friends over. At such times, it was beyond Cook to manage the fare alone so I got actively involved.

Charles was kept very busy with his writing. I was so proud of him. He made a lot of money but more important, he had become a highly respected writer. I read all that he wrote, though mostly after it was printed.

Charles had befriended Forster a few years ago and they had become very close friends. Charles trusted

Forster implicitly and gradually Forster took over the task of dealing with Charles' publishers and also reading his manuscripts. I liked Forster and very soon he was part of our family. His birth date was the same as our wedding date and we celebrated the day by having lunch together. Forster is still a part of the family, only I am not in it anymore. He acted for Charles in our separation.

Other new friends were the Macreadys. They were much older to us but we got along very well and often dined together. Mrs. Macready's given name also was Catherine. We were on the friendliest of terms. She succumbed to illness a few years before my separation. I wonder what she would have made of it? Would she have sided with Charles like her husband did? I think if she was alive, she would have convinced him to champion my cause.

By now, Charles had authored *Pickwick Papers, Oliver Twist, Nicholas Nickelby, The Old Curiosity Shop, Barnaby Rudge,* and also written stories and articles in the newspapers. He worked very hard, especially during the period when he was writing episodes of Oliver Twist and Nicholas Nickelby simultaneously.

But his energy was tremendous and he showed most of us to a disadvantage. He rode, swam, and went for long walks. Whether we were at home or holidaying somewhere, he invited troops of friends and my heart swelled with pride when I saw how he shone in any company.

Charles also met with astounding success on the other side of the Atlantic. He was delighted; he had a great fondness for America and American values. When he received invitations to visit America, he decided he would take a break from writing and go, and I would accompany him.

I did not want to go. Nor did I want him to go. The voyage could be difficult and there were the babies to think of. Charley was about five, Mamie three, Kate two, and Walter had not completed his first year.

But Charles was adamant. The children would be looked after; he would make arrangements. He needed the break from writing and the trip would serve him well. Macready added his voice to Charles and as usual, I could not hold firm against persuasion. I was made to see that my place was beside my husband, for whom this trip was very important; it was a great honor bestowed upon an Englishman.

We made arrangements for the care of the children in our absence. We hired three nurses and a governess, Charles' brother Fred moved in and the Macreadys promised to be always at hand, and keep a watchful eye.

Yet my distress at being away from the children was great. Our friend, Daniel Maclise, made a drawing of my children playing together, and gave it to me. It was a very good likeness, and during our trip to America, the picture was always beside my bed, no matter where we went.

We left for America on 4th January, 1842. Charles told me it would be a short visit but we were away for six months, returning on 29th June.

Our trip to America was a great success. Charles was accorded a welcome befitting royalty. He was much admired and hosted but both of us soon wearied of the crowds and the lack of privacy. Yet, we recaptured the days of our courtship. I was not tied down with the children and the household, he was not surrounded by friends and editors, he had no deadlines to meet, and because of practical considerations, we did not want another babe on the way. So we spent more time talking, and found a great deal of comfort in each other's company.

For all the pleasantness of the trip, there was nothing like the joy of returning home, and being reunited with the children. How happy we were! Charley was so happy he became ill. No amount of kisses to the children would suffice, and I hugged the children so much that Kate complained I was hurting her.

How had Charles forgotten those days? Why did he say I never loved my children, and had put up a show for the sake of Miss Coutts?

NINE

Mesmerizing, As Usual

C harles shot into fame soon after our marriage. He made new friends, both from the world of letters and from the theatre. Some of them led questionable lives, I knew, but I entertained them as they were Charles' friends.

Charles was revealing himself to be different from the man I had thought him to be. He was very controlling and not very loving, unless it suited him. He was not averse to disparaging me or the children to his friends. He was insensitive and even brutal, but I did not reproach him. Was I a saint? No. I was just a woman who wanted a stable marriage, who was by nature peace- loving, and who disliked scenes.

Charles was always impatient of my pregnancies. Being very energetic, he never understood why I found it necessary to rest so often. Childbirth and miscarriage debilitated me, but Charles thought I could be up and about if only I would.

I was again pregnant in June 1843. It was a year since Georgina had come to live with us. She came visiting when we returned from America. Fifteen and just out of the schoolroom, and happy to romp and play with the children, her visit continued longer than expected.

She was now sixteen and totally devoted to Charles. When he told her he could trace many of Mary's mental faculties in her, she was delighted. For her it was high praise to be told by Charles that her presence brought back the times when Mary lived with us.

Charles was very busy after our return from America. He also grew irritable. His latest serial, Martin Chuzzlewit, was not doing as well as he expected. There were demands, monetary demands, from his parents and brother. While expenses grew, his earnings had fallen.

Devonshire Terrace was a big house, and expensive. Charles conceived the idea we would live in France for a while. It would be cheaper and he would work better. I did not agree. There was a baby on the way. We could live in England, and take a smaller house, I said. But Charles had made up his mind. He saw life on the Continent as healthier, and more suited to him for writing.

As usual, he was inflexible. "Kate, you must exert yourself. Living in France will do everyone good. The baby will not be a problem. You can leave him with your mother."

I did not want to leave my child behind. I had just endured a long separation from my other children. For once, I was firm and Charles had to listen.

During this time, Charles wrote *The Christmas Carol*, the book that would start his Christmas stories.

Our Christmas that year was wonderful. I was close to my confinement. Francis would be born twenty days later. Though Cook tried to make me rest, I personally supervised the cooking and when the preparations were made, I sat in the midst of my family, wrapped in the glow of the festival and the warmth of love.

On Boxing Day, Mrs. Macready gave a children's party. Charles and Forster did conjuring tricks and they were better than the regular performers.

Twelfth Night, which was also Charley's birthday, was always celebrated in our home. The Twelfth Night cake, with the bean and the pea, grew in size as the number of our family and friends grew. That year, to our immense delight, Charles and Forster repeated their conjuring act for us.

Francis was born ten days later. Charley found his younger brother 'queer', Mamie wanted to cradle him, Kate wanted me to put him to sleep and listen to her and Walter did not like me to hold him. He cried until I handed Francis to the nurse and took him in my lap.

It hurt that Charles did not visit the new baby often. He behaved as if the baby did not exist. This was to become the norm for all the births that followed. The miscarriages did not count at all. Perhaps he considered them good riddance.

Everyone agreed he was a very good father, and he was. But the children interested him only after a certain age and that too, if they fit the mould he created for them. Charles was not different from many other men, though he believed otherwise.

He was still insistent about moving to France. As I could not travel immediately, he postponed our trip and went to Liverpool, on a speaking assignment. He was an excellent speaker and his speech to a thirteen hundred strong audience was a great success.

At Liverpool, Charles saw Christiana Weller play the piano and he was totally smitten. She was beautiful, talented; my own father had written a glowing review about her performance.

He told me in a nonchalant manner about the effect she had on him, "I could not look away from her, she was beautiful. It was as if she was the only person there and I followed her each movement, I can't forget her, Kate, I will always remember her."

He was very clever, he thought if he spoke frankly of his admiration, I would not guess at his infatuation. He had not stopped at admiring her; he had gone to her house uninvited, and presented his personal copies of Tennyson's poems to her.

"Thomson should marry her," he told me. Thomas Thompson was his friend, he was a rich widower. "Any man would be lucky to possess her and he is free." How innocent it all was. Yet, when he praised her, it was as a lover would, and it was with a regret that he himself was not free to pursue her. He was clearly infatuated and it only ended when Christiana married Thomson.

He often used openness as a smokescreen for his real thoughts, to delude others and perhaps even himself. He would have found it unbelievable that his dull, unimaginative wife knew him so well. We need not be blind to be in ignorance of what takes place around us; we have only to shut our eyes to achieve the same result. As I did.

What did I say when he praised beautiful Christiana Weller? What did I do? Nothing, except to feel ugly and unattractive, and jealous.

I had given birth to his child a few weeks ago, a child he showed scant interest in, and he had thoughts only for the beautiful Christiana, who reminded him of Mary, "*I saw an angel's message in her face that day that smote me to the heart,*" he said.

Was I being fanciful? I sometimes chided myself. Charles was a busy man, with varied interests, and as his wife, it was my duty to support him. But now, after my marriage has been disrupted by Ellen, I realize Charles has always been violently attracted to young girls on the threshold of womanhood. Instead of admitting it and curbing this tendency, he put them on a pedestal, and turned his carnal sentiments to something sublime. With a lot of time for introspection and for dissecting my marriage and my husband's character, I've come to this understanding. This knowledge is, of course, of no use to me now.

We went to Genoa in the middle of July, 1845. Charles wanted me to leave Baby Francis with my mother but I convinced him otherwise. Along with Georgy, whom Charles called his 'little pet', the four children, the baby, nurses and maids, we moved to the Continent to set up a home.

By September, Charles had rented a grand old palace, very cheap but very grand, with frescos and sculptors and fountains. The views from the palazzo were breathtaking, especially of the sea, and all of us, adults and children alike, went from window to window, exclaiming over them.

The weather was fine, not cold like England, and we spent a lot of time on the terraces of the palazzo. Charley yelled like a trooper, running in the corridors with Kate at his heels. Kate was growing into a handful and exhibiting a mind of her own. Charles called her his Lucifer Box. Mamie was easier to manage, you only had to tell her she would please her Papa if she behaved in a certain way, and she obeyed.

Francis passed all the interesting baby stages at the palazzo. He crawled, and took his first steps there. He was so funny and adorable, that Charles could not stay untouched. Soon he had named him 'The Chickenstalker'.

Though Charles was busy writing, yet he had time enough to be lazy with us. He made some new friends, Emile De La Rue and his English wife, Augusta, but I did not take to them. Worse, I thought them frauds and even immoral. This made Charles cool towards me; he was used to having me as a sympathetic listener but I would not listen to him speak about the De la Rues. The mere mention of the Swiss and his wife would annoy me.

Augusta was an attention seeking woman, the type who have more to say to men than woman. I did not like her husband either. I told Charles, "I don't think much of Madame De La Rue. Though she tries to be charming, I think she is a little vulgar."

"I think she is a charming woman, and shows courage in her affliction."

"What affliction?"

"She has a nervous disorder. She is subject to terrible headaches, suffers from insomnia, and convulsions. I told her husband about Elliotson, and his treatment using mesmerism."

"And?"

"They can't go to England to see Elliotson. When Emile learnt I've some skill with mesmerism, he and Madame asked me to try and cure her."

"But Charles, you are not a doctor!"

"I could send you and Georgina into trances, remember? Mesmerism is nothing but imposing my will on a weaker person's. I'm sure I will manage to get to the

67

root cause of Madame De La Rue's ailment. In fact I'm quite looking forward to it."

It was true Charles had mesmerized me. He first did it during our trip to America and made me hysterical. I remember how powerless it had made me feel.

He was so excited about trying out his powers that he started the treatment two days before Christmas. I tried to get him to postpone it. He had just returned from a month long of travel, and the children and I were looking forward to spending time with him. The festive season was not the same without his presence. We were like planets and he was our sun, shedding light and warmth.

But whenever Charles was caught up in a new idea, it was impossible to deter him from his path. He commenced his treatment. He frequented the De La Rue establishment, a pretty apartment on the top of a pallazo. The flights of stairs did not deter him from dashing to Madame's aid whenever Emile sent word.

Charles brought me news about his 'treatment'. Augusta was responding well, he told me. She would go into a trance and he would question her. She was even sleeping better after only a month of his ministrations.

I just wished he would finish with the sessions and get busy with something else. My reason was not only the association with De La Rues that I disliked, but he told me he had experienced her 'demons'.

In the middle of January, Charles decided to take me to Rome; the children and Georgina would stay in Genoa.

This was to be our holiday. We would see the carnival.

We took in the pretty sights, visited the churches, and spent happy times together as a couple. Charles sometimes worried about a break in Madame's treatment. He was delighted when the De La Rues came to Rome in March and moved into the same hotel as us.

Madame was very ill almost as soon as they moved in. Staying in the same hotel had its advantages. Her husband had to only knock on our door and Charles would rush out, full of solicitude. Sometimes he would stay away most of the night, treating Madame, and I would spend the hours awake, alone in the strange hotel room.

He never apologized for his absence. Instead, he explained to me the terrible suffering his patient underwent. She had great seizures and would lie unconscious, he explained, and such spells lasted for hours. He was able to give her relief, sometimes within an hour, while hitherto her spells had lasted for as long as thirty hours.

One night when the summons came, I was still in my day clothes. I had been sick and felt uneasy. I knew I would not be able to sleep so I asked to accompany Charles and he agreed.

I was unprepared for what I saw. Augusta De La Rue was dressed in a sleeping robe and because she was curled up tightly, the robe had slipped up. Her long hair was unbound and spread over her and hid her face.

Charles, with what looked like practiced ease, combed back her hair with his fingers, massaging her scalp as he did so. He smoothed his hand over her face, kneaded her neck, and rubbed her hands. She lay insensible. He murmured, nay, crooned to her, asking her questions about what she saw and whom.

Emile stayed in the room for a little while and went to sleep in another room. Charles continued his treatment, unceasingly moving his hands in what I could only describe as languid caresses. I watched the ceaseless moving of his fingers as he bent over her, trying to hear what she mumbled. I quietly left. Charles did not notice me leave.

When he returned to our room in the morning, he faced not the docile Kate he was used to but a virago. I was furious with him and lashed out at him for his improper behavior. I would not let him get a word in. I even threw his infatuation for Christiana in his face. "You were sighing for her until you started on Augusta!"

Charles was taken aback. He was not prepared for the attack. He also knew there was truth in my words. But my fury ended in a burst of tears.

"Kate, darling, what is it? I swear I've never dishonoured you!" he said, putting his arms around me.

"What else do you think, I'm pregnant! I've been constantly sick and you don't even notice because you are busy playing doctor elsewhere."

I felt Charles stiffen. His arms fell away from me. He went to sit at the table, dropping his head in his hands. "Not again!" he murmured. "Why do you have to spoil everything by getting pregnant? I don't want another child. Already I feel a shadow on our coming days."

My fury returned. I marched to him and shook him, hard. "I get pregnant? Are you out of your mind? What have you been doing since we came to Rome? Is that not how babies are made?"

He stared at me, shocked. We never spoke about our intimacies.

The rest of our days in Rome passed in sullen silence from his side and coldness from mine. He still went to treat Madame whenever he was called and as I refused to speak to him, he discussed his healing when we had company, and told me obliquely about the great good he was doing to the suffering woman.

I was relieved to leave Rome. We visited Naples and Florence before returning to Genoa. By the time we returned, though I had not forgiven him, I was on cordial terms with him again. It could not be otherwise, with Georgina, the servants and the children around. Moreover, the marriage bed could not be avoided for long; didn't the husband have his rights? Rights that resulted in duties for the wife?

The De La Rues also were back in Genoa. Charles was visiting them again, training Emile in the art of mesmerism, he told me stiffly, but I pretended not to hear. I did not want to make another scene; I already regretted my behavior in Rome. I knew then, as I know now, in Augusta's case, Charles was more attracted by the idea of having power over her mind, rather than on her. In the process she had become very dear to him but I still thought the whole exercise improper. When we left for England in June, Augusta gave Charles presents -a purse, a glass, slippers - and took an extremely fond farewell from him.

Charles treasured the gifts, whether in remembrance of the giver or as an annoyance to me, I never knew.

Charles never liked to be found in the wrong. Over the years, he even believed he could never be in the wrong. Some months after our return to England he told me, "Emile and Augusta expected me to visit this month. They are severely disappointed I did not go. They had a room prepared and my favorite dishes planned."

"Why did you not go?"

"You know why. I didn't want to be the subject of your insane jealousy. There was no basis for your behavior in Rome and you know it."

"It was improper behavior by any standard, Charles, and you know it."

"How was it improper? I was not alone with Augusta in Rome."

"The night calls were improper. You stayed with her while her husband slept in another room."

"No one would have thought it improper. You were staying in the same hotel. I was doing the sessions with your full consent and knowledge."

"I never gave you consent!"

"Of course you did, until that scene you created. You should have stopped me in the beginning. Their hopes would not have been raised, they would not have come to Rome. You owe them an apology."

It was useless to speak further. Then, as now, my being unable to change his mind was tantamount to giving consent. Yet, who could change his mind? No one I know of. Forster, Macready, Georgina, everyone yielded to his stronger will. Even before dabbling in the art of mesmerism, Charles had a mesmerizing personality.

TEN

The Last Straw

I've been living in this house on Gloucester Crescent for more than a year now. The house bears witness to my frenzies of grief, my spells of depression, my rages against Charles, and my piteous tears for my children.

I've lived alone for a year. What had seemed like an impossibility has come to pass.

When I was alone the first night since moving in, I had remained awake the entire night. I had listened to the sounds of the street until they fell silent and then I had heard the sounds within the house. An innocent creak, a shuffle, and I lay waiting for the next sound. The clock struck the hours through the night and I counted them all. I spent the night awake and alert, without a thought or tear for my former life, and lived every second of my solitude.

The tears came at dawn; tears and dangerous, unchristian ideas of taking my own life.

The nights after that were never that terrible. I still spent many of them awake but I remembered the past, both happy and sad, and worried about my future and that of my children.

I often wondered whether Charles thought of me. If I had not found the bracelet, and protested, would we have separated? I am convinced we would have; he would have found a way.

Helen visits me often. She is a sensible young woman, and devoted to me. She hates Charles for what he has done. With her, I can be myself. I can laugh or cry, or snap. She is annoyed with me on only one count: I do not hate Charles all the time.

One morning, I was reminiscing about the time when Charley had fallen ill with scarlet fever. He was in school in England, and the rest of us were in Paris. The school sent him down but though Charles and I rushed to be by his side, the doctor forbade us to see him. I was pregnant and scarlet fever could harm me and the unborn child. While my mother and Helen nursed Charley, I worried over my first-born.

Though he had much more to bear, Charles was like a rock of support during those terrible days. His sister had consumption, he was under pressure from his editors for meeting deadlines, but he managed everything. I couldn't have got through those days without his support.

He was good with the children when they were young, and he was their favourite. When Kate fell ill, she refused to be nursed by anyone but him. Mamie always wanted to please him and he gave her particular praise.

Those days Charles would worry about money, I told Helen. He had seen hardship in his childhood and was unsure whether he would make enough from writing serials. He decided it was better to have a regular job and signed up as editor of Daily News.

Within a short time, he was unhappy with his decision. We spent long hours discussing the issue and finally decided he would quit the paper. As a measure of economizing, and also to help Charles concentrate on his writing, we again went to Europe in May 1846. Our family had grown by another son, Alfred, who was born in October of 1845.

We lived in Lussanne during the summer months and moved to Paris in winter. He commenced writing Dombey and Son in Lussanne. The opening chapters were so moving, especially when Charles read them aloud, that I had tears running down my face.

Charles was ill during this time. He was having spells of giddiness and sick headaches. I accompanied him to Geneva, where he recovered. What really helped, I believe, was the success of Dombey and Son.

We returned to England in March 1847. Sydney was due to be born in April. It proved to be a most difficult and painful birth. Charles panicked and rushed for a second doctor. When the ordeal was over, he held me close for a long time.

As it sometimes happens, I had slipped so much in the past that I was recollecting Charles with fondness. I realized what I was doing when Helen left me in a huff.

Charles had always been demanding, even controlling and insensitive to the feelings of others but in many ways, he was admirable. He genuinely felt for the poor and did not hesitate to involve himself actively in charity. I remembered his writing and his concentration, and his delight when he made someone laugh or cry with his stories. He was a wonderful writer and possessed a magnetic personality. He was capable of much laughter, and often made the people around him come alive.

Why had he become so cruel, so unfeeling? When I lived with him as his wife, I would not have believed he was capable of such heartless behaviour. He was truly noble and gave of himself generously to his friends.

We had our quarrels and we made up too, like husbands and wives do. He had his peculiarities, his excessive neatness and his wish to arrange everything the way he wanted, they exasperated me while my inclination for a more homely arrangement instead of everything stiffly formal annoyed him. I found his excessive energy made me feel restless, he found my leisurely way of taking walks stifling. But these were differences we were used to. We joked about them to our friends and to each other. These were differences common to many households. They were not the cause of the breakdown of our family.

I had been sure it was Ellen but Charles had inserted a public notice that read like an oath, that she was not the reason for our marital troubles.

What then had caused this sudden turnabout? It was not a gradual change but a sudden one when he moved out of our bedroom. Or was it so gradual that I hadn't seen it?

The old suspicion came again. Was Charles suffering from an ailment? Was it a mental disorder we were unaware of, he was unaware of? If that was the case, he needed my love and care because he didn't know what he was doing.

The more I thought about Charles and contrasted his present behavior with his past one, the more I was convinced he was not in his senses. I sent for Charley.

"Charley, your father is unwell," I told him as soon as he entered.

"Did someone send word?" he asked, immediately alarmed.

"No but Charley, think! His behavior is insane. I thought he destroyed our home because he was infatuated by the actress. Better men than him have lost their heads over young women. But he swore she was not responsible and Charley, I believe his statement. I know what is wrong! He is suffering from a mental ailment and that is causing his inexplicable behavior. You told me yourself his behavior is that of a mad man. The girls keep out of his way. Charley, your father is in no condition to think properly and Georgy is of no use. She can never decide anything. She does whatever Charles wants her to and he is no longer rational. Charles needs me, I must go to him. Oh my poor darling, what will happen to him?"

While I was speaking, I was tying my bonnet strings.

Charley gripped my hands tightly and restrained my movements. He was looking at me with pity in his eyes but his face was set in harsh lines.

"No, you are not going anywhere. Not now, not ever. Promise me."

"Charley, why..what?"

"He is insane but not in the way you think. I've seen them together. His high sounding disclaimers in the papers were made to hide a sordid truth. He has been keeping Ellen Ternan and her family, and has purchased a house for them. Mother, when you were weeping in Tavistock House, hoping he would come to you, he was already making gifts of money to Ellen Ternan. I've a friend in the bank. I got a statement of his account made recently. It shows payments of money made to Ellen Ternan and to her mother, Fanny Ternan."

"Charley, could it be charity? They are poor, and Fanny Ternan is an actress, who is not able to get much work. Your father has helped families of destitute actors in the past," I asked, clutching at straws.

Charley did not answer and continued to hold me. Both of us knew Charles generated funds for needy actors by putting up plays and soliciting funds and not secretly from his bank account.

Charley left. So it was true after all, I thought, as my hopes crashed. I remembered a sentence from Dombey and Son, *"It is when our budding hopes are nipped beyond recovery by some rough wind, that we are most disposed to picture to ourselves what flowers they might have borne if they had flourished."*

ELEVEN

Darkest Night

Ellen Ternan, who was no older than our third child Kate, was my husband's mistress! I let the bitter and unpalatable truth sink in, as Charley left the house.

I had suspected as much and confronted Charles with the evidence of the engraved bracelet. He had burst into righteous anger, and later, when I told him I was prepared to listen to him, to believe him if he would explain, he had rushed away to the lawyers, to carve me out of his home and life.

Charles had a fascination for the stage. He had wanted to be an actor before he met with flattering success as a writer. He would have been a good actor, too.

He was quite familiar with the theatrical world. He had close friends from the theatre. In his early days as a reporter he spent a lot of time with actors and playwrights. He was an active member of Garrick's Club, a place where writers and actors socialized. He knew about the pitiful lives of actresses, as he knew about seamstresses who were forced to walk the streets, and he was always sorry for them. He did not look down upon them but pitied them as castaways from a social system that simultaneously preyed upon them.

Charles was so fond of acting that for many years he was involved in amateur theatre. He had converted the huge schoolroom at Tavistock House into the 'Smallest Theatre in the World.'

He wrote a play, 'The Frozen Deep', along with his friend Wilkie Collins. A year before I was removed from my home, that is in 1857, Charles decided he, along with family and friends, would stage the play for Charley's birthday, which fell on Twelfth Night.

Charles was writing *The Little Dorrit* at that time. He was so excited about putting up *The Frozen Deep* that he hired workers and carpenters who prepared the stage to represent the North Pole.

Mamey, Kate, Georgy, all acted in the play but the star performer was Charles. The play was well received by friends so when an opportunity arose for putting it up commercially, Charles grabbed it. The only change made was, naturally, he took professional actresses instead of girls from the family so as not to expose them to a theatre going public.

Ellen, along with her sisters and mother joined the group. The play was to be at Manchester.

All of us went to Manchester along with the company of *Frozen Deep*. I remember the day we took the train for Manchester; it was on the morning of 20 August, and we boarded at Euston.

Charles, who was naturally the manager, with his usual flair for organizing things, had reserved several carriages in the train and also rooms at a grand hotel. The whole party of family, friends, and actors was looked after as if guests at a pleasure outing. But that did not mean Charles was not serious about the play. He put everyone hard to work.

The play was a great success and instead of the two scheduled performances, was staged thrice. Charles was elated and would speak of nothing else for days. He was all praise for the Ternan family. Ellen's part was small, and Charles did not speak of it. He praised her sister Maria's performance.

He did not make it obvious but, with a wife's instinct, I had noticed his regard for Ellen. I was glad we would not have anything more to do with them. Though the girls were well behaved, I found something cold and calculating about the mother, not that I blamed her for it; her life must be a difficult one.

In the course of conversation with them, Georgy learnt they would be performing at Doncaster next. I did not pay attention; it was not significant to me.

In the days that followed, Charles was either highly charged, talking about the play and particularly the

Ternans, or restless and irritable. I couldn't understand his changed behavior.

Like in any other big household constituting children, nurses and maids, Charles and I were incapable of a private conversation during the day. It was only after we went to bed that we had our discussions about the children, Charles' plans, and even our arguments.

After Sydney's birth, which was an extremely painful one, there were three more births, the last one of dear Plorn, in 1852. We were older now, and wiser in the ways of containing our family.

I looked forward to our nightly talks. Charles always liked to sound out his ideas. When he was away from home, he did so by way of letters and when he was home, we would talk.

After Manchester, Charles stayed away from me. I didn't notice at first; I thought he was catching up on his work. One night, I happened to be awake when he came in. It was very late and he expected me to be asleep. As he slipped into bed, he sighed deeply. It was so unexpected that I asked him what the matter was.

"Nothing, except that I've been feeling restless, and confined."

"By what?"

He made a vague gesture, "By this, this life, I suppose."

"You have a wonderful life, Charles."

"I knew you wouldn't understand. You are so calm and placid and..listless. Many times I think we are not suited."

Before I could answer him, he had turned over.

He left for a walking tour with Wilkie Collins. He did not tell me where he planned to go, which was unusual for him, but I learnt later he was at Doncaster, and had watched the Ternans perform. As Charles' fascination with the stage was nothing new, I assumed he was in the vicinity and had gone to see the Ternans on stage.

Nevertheless, I was worried about his behavior at home. He was troubled, yet excited. And his words about us not being compatible, why had he said that? I wished I could speak to someone about his changed looks but there was no one except Georgina and she would treat any remark about him as a criticism and jump to his defense.

Over the years, she had become obsessed by the idea that she was indispensible to Charles, that she alone could carry out his wishes. She had become annoying in her zealous care and I tried not to speak to her about him. She was my sister and lived with me yet our relationship had lost its warmth.

I did not tell Georgy anything.

One day I heard my maid Anne outside my door. Georgy was questioning her about something and asking her whether Charles had ordered the changes. I could hear fragments but did not come out. What could they be talking about? Anne was saying that 'Madame should know about this' while Georgy was insisting, 'Master would have told her had he wanted her to know. You carry out his instructions.'

I soon learnt, to my shock, what these instructions were. Charles wanted to convert the small dressing room into his own bedroom. There would be no connecting door. The door was being partitioned off by a bookcase for which Charles had sent meticulous instructions, as he had for the single bed.

I could not make anything out of this. He had told me nothing. We had always shared a large double bed. During our travels he always insisted on a double room. What had happened? Why had he changed after returning from Manchester?

Everything fell into place. It had to be the Ternans, the youngest daughter. I had seen him cast tender glances at her. I had casually questioned him also. Was that why he had stopped coming to our bedroom?

Though I knew this was his way of avoiding any confrontation, the suddenness and totality of his action alarmed me. It also shamed me as a woman. He was letting it be known he did not want me as his wife any longer. The younger children thought it was a game when the single bed was brought for his room but I could not look my daughters and my older son in the eye. Facing the servants was still more shameful.

I was shattered. It spelled to me his total rejection. I wanted him back like the comfort of an old blanket. Since six years, Charles had learnt contraception and we were practicing it. There was no longer the anxiety of more births. The passion of our earlier years had dimmed but our marriage bed gave him pleasure and me, warmth and comfort.

I could not sleep after Charles moved out. It was not as if I was not habituated to sleeping alone in the huge bed; I slept alone when Charles travelled but this was different. Every night I lay awake well past the time the house fell silent. I listened to the tread of his feet. Had he come in? Was he in the room next door? Was he asleep? Was he missing the easy comfort of our marriage but too stubborn to admit it?

Was he punishing me for my suspicions? Since Rome, he always said I was unreasonably jealous. Had I gone too far suspecting his intentions to a woman as young as his daughter? Was this his answer? I knew he could be quite unforgiving.

On the third night, when I heard him enter his room, he seemed to be in high spirits. He was talking and laughing with Georgina outside the room. I had my ear glued to the door. After Georgina left, I waited until I was certain everyone had retired for the night. I went to the bookcase which had been the connecting door and listened. I could hear faint sounds coming from the room. Charles was not asleep.

I went out and softly tapped on his door and waited. There was silence. I tapped again and said, "Charles, open the door. I know you are awake."

The door opened suddenly and Charles stood, furious.

"What is it?" he asked, raising his voice.

"Ssh, I want to speak to you," I answered, hoping no one would wake up. He was my husband but already I felt I was doing something shameful by seeking him out in his bedchamber.

He stood unyielding for a minute and then pulled me inside the room. I collapsed on his bed, that single bed he had ordered for himself.

"Charles, I'm sorry. I should have trusted you. I didn't mean anything about the Ternans except that you were giving them very particular attention and they are actresses. They could have misconstrued. The mother is very sharp. She may try to trap you and your reputation will be tarnished."

"Catherine, I will not hear a word against those virtuous ladies."

"They are a family of travelling actresses, Charles, you will call them virtuous and cast me aside! You have often told me stories of women in such positions and how many of them are easily seduced. You know their world. I can understand if you pity them but your defending them as virtuous ladies is a bit over the top!"

"Have you come to quarrel?"

"How can you say that, Charles? You know I never quarrel. You were to say I was sweet tempered."

"Catherine, once again, why have you come?"

"Am I not supposed to, Charles? I am your wife."

"What do you want?"

"What do I want? Charles, you have moved out of our room without giving me any reason. I want you to come back. Or at least tell me why you have moved out."

"Catherine, even you can't be so obtuse. Why do you think I barred the door and got a single bed?"

"Kate....you were to call me Katey or Kate. I was your darling Kate. Sometimes I was vexed with you because you would always persist in your attentions and when I started increasing, you would blame me, though not always in words."

"I will leave you alone now on, Catherine. You should be happy."

"No Charles, you know as well as I do I've always done my duty to you in the marriage bed. I've never denied you. Even when I was with child and unwell, I did not bar you. I want to know, I've a right to know why you don't want me."

Charles avoided looking at me and turned his face away.

Suddenly I knew. "It is a woman, isn't it? You are finding pleasure elsewhere."

I should not have said that. Charles did not like to be questioned. But my heart was breaking. My husband, my lover had turned away from me. I could not keep quiet.

Charles stuck his face close to me and grasped my arm so hard that his fingers left their imprints.

"And do you blame me?" he snarled. "Look at yourself! You have neither beauty of form nor mind. You are coarse and jealous and I'm heartily sick of you."

I stared at him and my jaw went slack.

"Look at you! You look like a lackwit!" he said in disgust and turned his back on me.

Indeed, I felt like a lackwit. How had I mistaken his intentions all these years?

"Sin..since when do you feel like this? I did not guess you were disgusted when you..." I broke down and wept with great shuddering sobs. I knew I should leave the room but my limbs would not move.

"Catherine, I am sorry I had to be harsh but this should not come as a surprise. You know we were never well suited. I am aware you have a genuine tenderness for me but we have only made each other unhappy, have we not?"

I did not lift up my head but I heard the implacable tone and knew if I looked up, I would find his big eyes staring into mine, mesmerizing me and his ceaseless words would convince me to think along with him. This is how it always was. He would decide something and talk me into believing that I wanted it. The children would want to attempt something and he would easily convince them to take the opposite course and they would follow, certain that this was what they wanted all along.

"Here, wipe your eyes and let me help you. You really *are* heavy!"

I stood near the door and looked at him. He was no longer angry. He even looked pleased with himself.

"You meant what you said, you will not return to our room?"

He sighed. "Catherine, Kate, you know in your heart we have moved away from each other."

"I know no such thing. We were fine a few weeks ago. Quarrels between husband and wife are commonplace but they do not make a spectacle of their marriage by making separate sleeping arrangements. What will the children and the servants think? What about Georgina?"

"Georgina understands and approves. I wrote to her when I was away. She agrees this arrangement will be for all our good."

"What has Georgy got to say in our marriage? How will it be to her good if you move out of our room? Unless she expects to move into yours."

"Catherine, you are slandering someone who has sacrificed the best part of her youth for us. She has been a mother to your children when you would not. You should touch the hem of her gown in gratitude. She has sacrificed herself to hold our home and marriage together."

TWELVE

Isolation

Of late, whenever I objected to anything Georgy did, Charles heard of it, it must be Georgy who told him, and he took me to task for being ungrateful to someone who had been a 'mother' to my children.

He would not listen when I pointed out that Georgy had not been a part of our household for the first five years. During the next eleven years, when I was often confined with the babies that came, we had nurses to look after the children, and tutors to teach them. We had a cook and maids and footmen. Georgy only started the children on their ABCs, though their nurses were capable of the simple task.

She did not sit with me during the long months when I lay in bed, with my feet propped up, and cushions behind my aching back. She did not help me when I was weak after I miscarried. At all those times, it was my maid Anne who cared for me.

With the servants and nurses doing all the work and taking care of the children, Georgina's presence was not needed in running the house but she managed to look busy. She would bustle about ordering the servants, and make a great show of following Charles' instructions. The children would be engaged with their nurses and she would suddenly gather them and engage them in some loud, boisterous game, especially when Charles was around.

I did not say anything though many times her behavior was annoying. By the time she was in her mid-twenties, Georgy had become bossy and tiresome.

She would ask to accompany Charles on his long walks, often saying words to the effect, "I'm sure Kate is feeling too lazy or Kate is a slow coach, she can't keep up with us." As long as Charles was home, she hovered around him, and was at his beck and call.

She found ways of pleasing him. If Charles placed a chair in a particular way, or commented upon the ornaments on the mantelpiece, she saw to it that the arrangement was repeated every day. She didn't stop at that but pointed out to Charles that dear Kate had forgotten but she remembered because it was necessary to have everything neat and orderly.

She was not tied down with work or pregnancy. The children had their nurses and she suffered them around her only when she wanted to. She was young, energetic, and was always free to attend to Charles. She made much of him, and though she wasn't really well read, she picked up his opinions and parroted them. Soon she was joining him and his friends in informal gatherings and even when he was alone, she sat with him in rapt attention or used her talent for mimicry in entertaining him.

There was a similarity between Georgina and Charles. Both did not care whom they hurt. It always surprised me how Georgina used her wit against me and did not seem to care that she drew tears. We had the same upbringing. She should have been too well bred to behave in this manner but I watched her change from a pleasing girl of fifteen to a hard woman who hid her malice well and was both hypocritical and self-serving.

I turned away from thoughts of Georgina and once again revisited that shameful night. When Charles had helped me up, he did not do so with any gentleness; his touch was one of hatred and disgust, as was his cruel remark about my being 'heavy'.

Hurt and angered I said, "Charles, if there is no place for me by your side or in your heart, why should I live here? You always make it a point to remind me that Georgy takes care of our home and children and she has a greater claim on both. If you believe that, I've no right to live here. I must leave this house and go away."

"Catherine, you always were prone to see the dark side of things. Many husbands and wives have separate sleeping arrangements. We are better than many others. We have a tender regard for each other, we can be friends. There are many kinds of love. We can love each other like brother and sister."

"After siring more children with me than you care to count, you will love me like a brother! Is that what you meant when you said you loved Mary like a brother?"

I quickly opened the door and stepped out. I was not very surprised to walk into Georgina. She did not seem embarrassed. Rather, she looked annoyed. She followed me into my room.

"Kate, you shouldn't have spoken to Charles like that! You know he is having trouble writing these days. As a wife, it is your duty to support him."

I wanted to retort that she as an unmarried woman would not know a wife's duty but I checked my angry words. Instead I asked, "How about a sister's duty? Was it not your duty to tell me Charles wanted a separate room?"

"How could I speak? That was between the two of you."

"And this isn't? Georgy, please leave. Better still, go to Charles as you understand him so well."

How does a child fare if it he is punished for no fault? Or a dog whipped by its master?

I was in the same condition. My anger gave way to fear and confusion. I did not know what I had done wrong. Charles had spoken to wound me and he had succeeded but I also knew he had spoken falsely. He had never come to me in disgust.

I did not leave my room until late in the afternoon of the following day. I listened to the sounds of my children.

Only Henry and Plorn were home; Walter was in India and the other boys were away at school. Charley, being a young man, had his own quarters. Kate and Mamie, though in the house, were silent.

Henry and Plorn were creating a racket, shrieking in imitation of a train. I heard Kate scold them and I heard Georgy laugh, I guessed the 'boy train' had crashed into her.

The maids did not come to my room. Like servants everywhere, they must know about the quarrel. If they needed orders, they would go to Georgy. Anyway, they preferred to go to her because she often countermanded my orders, which meant extra work.

I tidied myself half-heartedly and left my room to eat. I heaped a plate with meat pie and kippers. After working through it I took a hearty slice of seed cake. The smell of newly baked bread came from the kitchen. I called a maid and asked her to bring the loaf and some cheese. After finishing half the loaf, I asked for chocolate. I knew I was eating more than I should but I couldn't stop myself. Food was comforting and it took my mind away from my sorrows. I had found solace in food earlier too, especially before and after childbirth, when I spent hours and hours alone in my room during my confinements.

I went back into my room and broke down again. I spent the hours up to dinner in my room and dozed off because of the sleepless night I had spent.

At dinnertime, one of the maids came to ask whether I would come down to dinner or have it in my room as everyone else had gone out. Georgina had asked the master for the boys to be given a treat and he had taken all of them out for dinner.

They must have left while I was asleep. The maid was looking at me, I thought, with pity. I put up a brave front and said, "I know they are not at home. Master told me. And yes, I'll eat in my room."

I finished the loaded tray but after a while, I was again hungry. I heard voices, happy voices of my family who had returned after having a good time. I heard the children go to their rooms, I heard everyone wish everyone else a good night, and I waited for someone to come in and enquire whether I had supped. I also waited, foolishly, for Charles to come in and apologise or make light of what he had said.

No one came and two hours later, in the darkness of the night, I crept with a candle into the kitchen and cut myself a big slice of cake and also took some pie. I ate as if I was famished since a week. But I needed something more, something that would help me sleep and take the pain away. I took a bottle of wine with me back into my cold, solitary bedroom.

I remember spending three days in this manner. No one came to see me except my maid, whom I asked to leave. I took my meals alone, and smuggled wine into my room.

On the third day of my isolation, I heard quick steps outside my door, followed by a timid knock. Before I could get up, Georgy was saying, "Plorn, no! You naughty boy! You are not to trouble your mother."

"I want Mama!"

I rushed to the door and opened it. Porn was struggling in Georgy's arms.

"Georgina, leave him!" I said.

She looked at me, my sister living in the same house, who had not bothered to come near me in the last three days. She said, "You look positively frightful, I declare! You will upset the child."

But Plorn had freed himself. He bounded towards me and I scooped him up in my arms. He gave me a resounding kiss and I took him into my room. I petted him to my heart's content. The child of my body, what did he care I was fat and ugly and my face, blotched and puffy! He was content to lie in the warmth of his mother's embrace.

But not for long. A maid came with Plorn's outdoor clothes. Everyone was going for a walk with Aunt Georgy. Would he come?

Plorn did not resist the inducement and I did not try to keep him back. I could have, with assorted boxes and table ornaments but I was too close to tears to try.

Plorn's visit to me had one fortuitous outcome. I realized the children did not visit me because they were kept away. My shutting myself up did not help because they would be told I was ill and resting. I braved the onslaught of curious eyes, especially those of the youngest maid, and stayed out of my room during the day.

I was bold enough to attempt this because Charles was away from home. I had a notion I could pick up the reigns of my household in his absence.

One peculiarity of our household was that Charles had the final say in everything, even the menu. Freed of his presence, I planned the menu, with treats for the children. Suddenly, it was important for me to hear them squeal with pleasure at my small surprises.

But when we assembled for dinner, I did not find one single dish I had asked for. Georgina smirked all through the meal and made comments to the children about their poor Papa who would be forced to eat some dreary meal while all his favorite dishes were on the table. Weak and spineless that I was, I could not ask the cook why she had not carried out my wishes. That night I confronted Georgy. "Why do you do this?' I asked. "Why do you keep my children away from me?"

"What do you mean?"

"I am not as foolish as you imagine me to be. Why did you send for Plorn for taking a walk in the middle of the day? You wanted to remove him from my room, is that not so?"

"Children need exercise. Walks are good for them but you will never understand. And you are a good one to talk about the children being kept from you. You locked yourself away in your room though you were not ill. I think you were not ill, seeing the hearty meals you were taking. The servants found it amusing, that you could *feed* in the present circumstances."

What could I say? Put like that, it did seem I was an indifferent mother. I knew I was not but I was never good at words in an argument. I always grew quite upset and tearful and it was only long after an argument was over that I recollected the points I could have made in my favour.

THIRTEEN

The Demons Return

During this period I did something else very painful. One night, not long after my quarrel with Charles, I stripped myself and examined my body with a looking glass. Was I as loathsome as Charles said he found me? My skin was still soft and supple, and I remembered Charles' ardent kisses of yore.

Since when had I become a grotesque ogre? He could have told me. I would have tried to lose weight and make myself attractive or done something, anything to make myself pleasing and if nothing else, I would have been prepared for this humiliation.

I knew I had lost my looks, especially after Henry's and Dora's births.

Henry was born in January 1849, when I was thirty-four. The birth had been a very difficult one, with the baby awkwardly placed. Charles had taken the difficult decision, and I had agreed, for the doctor to use chloroform, which was recently introduced.

Dora was born on 15 August 1850. Dora's birth was relatively easy, the terrible ordeal lay in her death when she was just eight months old. She was a beautiful child, and a happy one. She was more precious to me, if that was possible, for she came after so many boys.

She fell ill when she was five months old but recovered fully. At that time I started to suffer with sick headaches. It was not a new condition, I had been suffering from migraine type headaches for three years but they were never so debilitating. Charles decided we would try the water cure at Malvern. He settled me in a comfortable house and left Georgie with me. The children were in the care of the nurses.

I could not know what misfortune lay ahead. A few weeks after I left, Dora suddenly had convulsions and died.

Charles sent Forster to bring me home. He could not tear himself from the house that held little Dora so still, when she had been active and playful a few hours before.

He was also worried about me. He wanted me to be composed for the sake of the children and for my own sake. He sent a letter with Forster. For all that Charles was a great writer, he was a father first, and he could not hide the truth in the letter.

My dearest Kate. (he wrote)

Now observe. You must read this letter, very slowly and carefully. If you have hurried on thus far without quite understanding (apprehending some bad news), I rely on your turning back, and reading again.Little Dora, without being in the least pain, is suddenly stricken ill. She awoke out of a sleep, and was seen, in one moment, to be very ill. Mind! I will not deceive you. I think her very ill.There is nothing in her appearance but perfect rest. You would suppose her quietly asleep. But I am sure she is very ill, and I can't encourage myself with much hope of her recovery. I do not—and why should I say I do, to you my dear!—I do not think her recovery at all likely.I do not like to leave home. I can do nothing here, but I think it right to stay here. You will not like to be away, I know, and I can't reconcile it to myself to keep you away. Forster with his usual affection for us comes down to bring you this letter and to bring you home. But I can't close it without putting the strongest entreaty and injunction upon you to come with perfect composure—to remember what I've often told you, that we never can expect to be exempt, as to our many children, from the afflictions of other parents—and that if—if—when you come, I should even have to say to you "Our little baby is dead", you are to do your duty to the rest, and to shew yourself worthy of the great trust you hold in them.If you will only read this, steadily, I've a perfect confidence in your doing what is right.

Ever affectionately,

Charles Dickens

I knew immediately little Dora was no more but I held myself in restraint until I reached Charles and when I was in his arms, only then I wept my heart out, and Charles shed his tears then.

He had seen me go through the difficult births, never far enough to recover my health or my looks, he had seen me age with the death of a beloved child, and yet he wanted me to look as beautiful and carefree as an eighteen year old. Dora died and within two months I was pregnant again with Plorn. My faded looks did not stop him then, neither did my ill health, but what was it that suddenly made him despise this body of mine? It had not changed much during the last few years.

And had I alone changed? When he sighed over an eighteen-year-old actress, did his glass not tell him he looked every day of his forty-five years?

In spite of my resentment at Charles' harsh words, I slowly, surreptitiously tried to cut down on food. I avoided rich food and tried to go for simple fare but I could never hold out for long. My control would break and I would gorge myself on food, and feel miserable. At those times, I hated my body, and more than that I hated Georgy, childless Georgy who had kept her figure and gained my children for herself too.

During the next few days I went out of the way to spend time with the children. Earlier, I would let them be if they were with their nurse or tutor.

Plorn always ran to me with some little surprise and asked me whether I was still ill. Mamie avoided me and stuck to Georgy. I tried to draw her out but she took her cue from Georgy in everything except she did not sneer like her. She was a young woman, grown enough to know her mind but she took a blinkered view of everything.

Guilt smote at my heart. Charles often blamed me for the lassitude and lack of direction in the children; he said their behavior was inexplicable until one surmised they took after me.

I looked at Mamie and tried to see myself in her. No, Mamie was not like me. At her age, Mary and I were quite open about our feelings. We indulged in simple pleasures and whiled away happy hours with our cousins. How had I not noticed Mamie's disposition before? Was it because she, like the rest of us, sparkled only when Charles was home?

Georgy's silences continued as did my status of an unwelcome guest in my own home. Charles kept himself aloof. It was as if he was laboring under some stress. The games and jokes that were a part of his presence were missing. Georgy kept announcing we should not disturb his work but I knew he was not writing; nothing could disturb him when he wrote.

Kate was the only one who continued to speak to me. I sensed some restraint in her which was to be expected because she was a grown woman and was aware of the rift between me and Charles. In her own sweet way she tried to bridge it by trying to bring me into her conversation with Charles but it only angered him.

Looking back, I wish I had made better use of that time. I should have taken Charley, Mamie and Kate into my confidence, to resolve the trouble that cast its shadow over our hitherto happy home.

For happy it had been! Though Charles denied it and said we were miserable, we had been content like many other families. Where we differed was in laying too much emphasis in pleasing one person, Charles, who was as easily displeased as he was pleased. We could bask in his praise one day and feel the frost of his disappointment the next day.

But I did not confide in my grownup children. I could not speak to them about my suspicions, they were shameful and moreover, I never believed our estrangement would be of a permanent nature. I was, after all, his wife of more than twenty years and the mother of his children. We had laid to rest a dear child, a veritable angel, and found comfort in each other. No, whatever this inexplicable coldness was, it would pass and while it was painful, Charles would revert to his teasing ways, sometimes embarrassing me in front of our friends but becoming solicitous if I was troubled. How I longed for those days because to be teased by Charles was to bear a special mark of his favor.

I took to spending more time with the boys. I also looked forward to the notes from my other boys in school, and from Walter.

I learnt that Charles had decided to pack Henry off to school. It was the middle of the term and Henry was only eight. I tried to speak to him but as usual he did not listen to me. I wondered whether the decision had something to do with the frequent 'disturbances' Georgy complained in Henry's lessons at home.

Henry went to school in the cold of December, leaving the house very empty. Two boys and their games can fill a mansion but a solitary boy in a household of women is quite lost.

Matters were the same between Charles and me. I never ventured to speak to him about the barrier he had constructed between us but I tried to reach across the wall of silence by uttering small, commonplace things.

Further disappointment lay ahead. Charles decided that the boys would not come home for Christmas but would spend it at school.

We did not have any of our usual festivities that Christmas. While many households on both sides of the Atlantic must have tried to celebrate Christmas in the spirit my husband made popular, he quenched the same from our home and hearth. It was a very sad and despondent Christmas and New Year.

Charles had not started another book. He was jumpy and irritable, and nothing pleased him. He was sometimes short with Georgy too. When he was home, he preferred to keep himself away or take solitary walks. He had always been fond of long walks and Georgy liked to accompany him but now he went alone and when he returned, he did not look happy but rather like a man labouring under a burden. I foolishly imagined he was troubled on account of our long drawn out estrangement. I thought he was stubbornly clinging to his pride but wanted a reconciliation and was as miserable as I was.

I know now he was disturbed because he was unable to come to any arrangement about Ellen. He had started helping the family but had not won the favours he wanted. I like to think it was not just the frustration but also the burden of guilt. He had always written about Christian values and goodness and believed himself to uphold them but during those months, he was lusting after Ellen Turnan, who was as young as Kate.

We continued as a sorry household during the coming months. Plorn was like a silent ghost, moping for his father and brothers, Mamie was often closeted with Georgy, Kate spoke to me but did not seek me out and I tried to put on a good front.

One such day, when I was sitting alone, the maid announced a delivery from a jeweler. My foolish heart leapt. I was sure the delivery was for me. To whom else could it be? It must be a peace offering from Charles, it was so like him to win me back with a surprise.

I opened the box with eager fingers and touched the pretty bracelet delicately. My tears, always so ready, filled my eyes. Dear, darling Charles. I opened the accompanying note.

It was addressed to Ellen Ternan, asking her to accept the small token of his affectionate regard. The jeweler had sent it over by mistake.

I went berserk. I threw the ornament across the room. By the time Charles came home, I was in a towering rage. I had been in agony, and yes, guilt for not pleasing my husband any longer, while the fault lay with him. He had put me aside because he had strayed.

I went into my room after flinging away the bracelet and waited for him, so angry I could do him physical violence. As soon as I heard him come in, I rushed into the passage, screaming, abusing. When I confronted him, he looked at me coldly, and said, "Have you lost your mind?"

I rushed to the corner where the bracelet lay, a pretty thing with Charles' name engraved within, "You have lost your mind! You vile, lecherous, hateful man! What is the meaning of this? And this?" I thrust the note into his hand.

When he didn't answer, I said, "You said they were a virtuous family, is this how they conduct themselves, by soliciting gifts from rich men?"

My words inflamed Charles. "Not another word! You know nothing, nothing! You have always been jealous, even of Mary. This is a simple gift, and you know I send gifts to people who work with me."

"Enough. You have fooled me enough! A gentleman does not send ornaments to single women unless he is sure they will be accepted and you know very well it is not proper for a woman to receive such gifts. If she is a proper young lady, as you insist, why are you sending this? And if it is because she worked in your play for three shows, hers was surely a minor part. Her sister and mother are more deserving of your attentions, your proper attentions. But your attentions are not proper, she is your mistress. Deny it if you can!"

Charles stormed out of the house. Kate stayed away. Mamie scuttled behind Georgina who pursed her mouth in disapproval. Hours later, Plorn alone crept into my room, bearing a sticky slice of cake. He wanted me to eat it. For his sake I tried but it was as difficult to swallow as a piece of stone.

After my burst of emotion, the house was silent. The youngest maid who always hummed could not be heard. The servants moved noiselessly, as did my children. Georgina alone behaved as if nothing was amiss. She called out to Plorn to practice his alphabet.

I was left alone, victor of a battle I never wanted and one I was not equipped to fight. I had never been able to cross Charles; he would never let me. Even in our early days of loving courtship, he had to have his way. He would even threaten me, indirectly, that he would break our engagement if I didn't do what he wanted. His will had only grown stronger during the years and mine, weaker.

I waited nervously, I did not know for what, and did not know how to approach Charles. Once again, the fight had gone out of me; I was prepared to accept whatever he told me, provided he promised not to see Ellen, and the estrangement of the last few months was bridged over.

When a maid came for me, with Charles' message to see him, I went eagerly. I had already decided to ask for his forgiveness. Shocking, isn't it, but I was used to his ways and knew until the fight was resolved, he would not let go of his anger. He would never admit his mistake, so it was best I pretended to believe him and leave it to his good sense to behave with propriety and honor.

"Catherine, I hope you have thought over your behavior and realized the injustice you have done to Miss Ternan. I know you see the need to visit them, and show them by your behavior that you think highly of them."

"Charles!" I wanted to remonstrate but he raised his hand for silence. "Catherine, I am not asking you to visit Mrs. Ternan because if you make the visit at my command, it would be valueless and contemptible, and have no value as an apology, even in your own eyes."

With these words, delivered in a cold voice, and with a colder look, Charles left the house, not before placing in my hands a scrap of paper with Mrs. Ternan's address.

I returned to my room and slowly donned my outside clothes. I tied my bonnet with nerveless fingers, and couldn't get it right. The strings seemed beyond me, in my present state. I started weeping.

Kate was passing by my room, she heard me and came in. "Mama, why?" she asked.

"Your father wants me to call on the Ternans."

"No! Mama, don't go."

"I'm going. I've sent them word to expect me."

Kate stared at me, nonplussed; she was old enough to know the nature of my quarrel with Charles and understood how humiliating the situation was for me.

I went to Park Cottage, Northampton Park, where Frances Ternan lived with her daughters, Fanny, Maria, and Ellen. I usually made good conversation while visiting out but this time, after the usual comments about the weather, an awkward silence hung over the small room. My eyes kept straying to Ellen, though I avoided looking at the bracelet she wore. Charles had found the time to send it, or had he come personally and prepared them for my visit?

Maria made a disastrous attempt to break the awkward silence. "Mr. Dickens has been very kind to us. He visited us when we were performing at Doncastor. He was very kind and amiable. He took us to the races, and he took Ellen in his carriage, on an expedition to the ruins of the Roche Abbey."

I looked at Ellen, who was fingering the bracelet. She did not look self-conscious in the least. I guessed she was still an innocent, and did not know where Charles' interests lay. In a way, it was strange because she and her sisters had grown up in the world of theatre, which was infamous for liaisons between rich patrons and actresses.

But Mrs. Ternan, *she knew.* I looked at her for a long moment, pleading with her to do what a mother should, and refuse Charles. Mrs. Ternan did not flinch from my look, and I read in her eyes calculation and victory. Wasn't I at her home, groveling forgiveness from my husband for no fault of mine?

I worried dreadfully, yet hoped Charles would come to his senses. I hoped my visit to the Ternans would prove to be abjection enough, and he would heal the breach.

But it was not to be. A few days later, Charles told me about his plans of separation. He also told Charley, who was as astounded as I was. Instead of speaking to his father, he wrote to him and said he would stay with me, his mother.

Charles moved out of Tavistock House, as did Georgy with the girls and Plorn, and I was left alone to take myself off, an unwelcome object.

FOURTEEN

Yet a Wife

Charley left, after awkwardly trying to comfort me, and I was glad he went. I did not need to restrain myself any longer. I shut myself in my room and pressing a cushion to my face, howled. I could not bear the agony; it slashed through me like a double edged sword.

I relived the pain of finding the bracelet, a tangible proof against my husband of twenty- one years; I smarted under the humiliation of the hour spent at Park Cottage under Mrs. Ternan's knowing eyes and, I remembered the confused hurt that filled my mind and heart when I read the disclaimer Charles had published in the newspapers. His statement had been so vehemently sincere, I was left wondering again whether he was really innocent, and wounded by my jealous outburst.

While Helen and my parents fumed that Charles showed scant consideration to my feelings, and was all concern for Ellen and her reputation, I was distressed whether I had driven him away, and was perhaps to blame for my sorry fate. How wrong I was! His protestations were a façade to preserve his reputation.

How was I so taken in? Why did I not recognize the smokescreen of words? I should have guessed, it was nothing new. Whenever he had something to hide, he protested too much and in the most convincing manner. There were incidents, shameful ones, when Charles, along with a friend, sought out women for pleasure.

When I grasped their innuendoes and asked him, he laughed uproariously as if I had been extraordinarily witty. 'What foolish notions you have! How many women do you think I've had? A hundred, a thousand, no, fifteen thousand is the number I would be satisfied with.' Over the years he turned it into a joke and repeated it to some friends that his wife was *'excruciatingly jealous of him, and had obtained positive proofs of his being on the most confidential terms with at least Fifteen Thousand Women.'*

Someone knocked on my door. Who could it be? The two servants I employed would not disturb me; they were accustomed to my locking myself in my room.

"Kate, it's me, Helen, open the door."

Why had Helen come at this time, was something amiss?

I hurried out of bed and opened the door. Helen entered my chamber; it was dark and cold as I had lit neither the fire nor the candles.

"What's the matter?" I asked, as Helen lit a lamp. She turned to me, took my face gently in her hands, and smoothed my hair away from my brow.

"Sit," she said, gently pushing me into a chair. She brought a wet washcloth and wiped me face, she undid my hair and combed it, and all this time she never said a word. Her sweet sympathy was too much to bear; I burst into fresh tears.

Helen left the room and returned with a tea tray. She prepared the tea and gave me my cup. After a few sips I asked, "Why have you come? It is quite late, almost bedtime."

"I came to spend the night with you."

"Why?" I asked but understood immediately. Charley must have asked her to come. He knew his confirmation about Ellen would have shattered me.

We had tea, and a slice of my mother's chocolate cake Helen had brought with her.

"I am sorry to have upset you," I told Helen, referring to our last meeting, when I had recollected the times Charles had been a caring and loving husband.

"No Kate, I was in the wrong. I had no right to ask you to shut out whatever gave you happiness in your life. The present is bleak enough, why should you not relive your past happiness? As a matter of fact, I insist that tonight we only speak of your happy years with your husband and children."

"Not tonight, Helen, not now, I cannot."

"You can, Kate, you are the bravest person I know. Anyone else in your place would have been in bedlam by now."

Helen made me smile with her words and her impersonation of a demented woman. "What is there to tell? You know everything that has happened to me."

"I do, but I want to hear it again. Tell me about the time after you returned from Paris."

"Let me remember, though I fear the events I recollect are always linked to births and pregnancies. We left for Paris in November 1846. You must remember Charles and I rushed back to England from Paris, because of Charley."

"Yes, I do. Charley had scarlet fever. You were pregnant so the doctor did not let you and Charles into the sick room. Mama and I nursed Charley, while you moped and worried."

"Yes, Charley still remembers you as a most tireless nurse. That was in February 1847. We returned to Paris after Charley was better. *Dombey and Son* did very well, and Charles made a lot of money. He told me confidently that we would never have to worry about money again."

"We had planned to live on the Continent until June. By then, I would be out of confinement and the new baby two months old. But Charles decided we would return to England sooner. *Dombey and Son* was doing better than expected, and he had some other plans. He was missing

117

his friends and London itself, as walking in its streets inspired much of his writing.

"There was also a family matter. His sister, Fanny, was suffering from consumption. He was very attached to her and though he had provided her with whatever care he could, he wanted to be close to her. We arrived in a great hustle and bustle. I was heavily pregnant, due to give birth within a month. We had let out our house at Devonshire Terrace up to the end of June so we needed to rent a house immediately."

"I remember," Helen said, "Mama was frantic about you. She thought it was not at all the thing for you to be crossing the channel in your state. She took Georgy to task, for instead of helping you she was bothering about trifles that Charles insisted upon, like placing the furniture in a certain manner. You were all to move out of the rented rooms in two months anyway. Mama thought it was more important for you to be settled comfortably first, rather than bother about chaises and table ornaments."

"Those were necessary, too. I was glad Georgy attended to arranging our things, as Charles could never spend even a single night in a hotel until everything was to his satisfaction. We were barely settled in and I was confined."

"That was your most difficult birthing, was it not? It was a breech birth. Come Kate, don't look at me like that. I am unmarried but what with you and my older cousins confined so many times, and Mama and my aunts discussing the complications of labor, I understand quite a bit. I know you had a very long labor, and the doctor thought you might not pull through. He said something about a breech birth. Mama immediately blamed it on Charles for the gallivanting he had made you do between London and Paris."

"How well you remember! Charles also was seriously alarmed, and he got a second doctor. Between them, they managed the birth and stopped the hemorrhaging. But it was such a terrible ordeal that many times I had wished to die. Poor Sydney, if he knew he had almost extinguished my life, would he come to me now?"

"He will, soon. Before you realize it, the boys will be grown men and worship you the way Charley does. Sydney was always an endearing child. He sometimes had such a wondering look on his face, as if everything fascinated him."

"Charles named him The Ocean Spectre, which soon got corrupted to Hoshen Peck."

"He was also called The Admiral, wasn't he?"

"Yes. Charles said he was a born sailor. Charley has been telling me Sydney will go to the Eastman Naval Academy soon."

I grew silent, remembering Sydney, and how he always held his own against his older brothers. But Helen had come with a mission tonight. She would not allow me to brood.

"You moved to your house in Devonshire Terrace soon after Sydney's birth, didn't you?" she asked.

"We moved in July. Charles was relieved to be working in his old study. While I recovered, he kept himself busy. He had too many rods in the fire. He was busy with The Home for unfortunate women. It was started in May, a month after Sydney's birth. The expenses were born by Miss Coutts but Charles did everything else. He finalized the premises, appointed the staff, and selected the inmates. He was tireless in his efforts. He really believed in the young women and wanted to give them an opportunity to change their lives. Many women who lived by wrong means gave up their way of life, learnt skills, and started new, respectable lives in the colonies.

"Charles was also putting together some theatrical production, to help Leigh Hunt who was in a bad way. As usual he was managing most of it himself. But he made time for his friends, for Forster and a few others, and continued with the popular *Dombey and Son*. He also took up some other social causes.

"When he returned home, and we retired for the day, he told me his plans and what he had accomplished. That had always been his way. When he was away from home, he would write long, chatty letters, and want me to do the same; when he was at home, he would talk late into the night. He had endless energy but after an intense spell of activity, he would suddenly take a break.

"In November we visited our friends from Lausanne, the Watsons, in their home in Northampton shire, Rockingham Castle. We left the children in the care of Georgina and the nurses; I was not keen to go but Charles wanted me to accompany him. Rockingham Castle was a picturesque place. It was built as a royal castle in the eleventh century and half destroyed in the Civil War. Its location was spectacular too; it was set high above a ravine. The undamaged part of the castle had been altered and built upon many times. What remained of the original castle was its great hall, gatehouse and round towers. We had a wonderful time there, not only because of the castle but because the Watsons were particular friends."

I stopped, remembering their friendship was lost to me; they had not contacted me after Charles left me. They knew me well, and also knew Charles' allegations were false, yet they had dropped my acquaintance.

Helen prodded me and I continued, though I knew she had no interest in my narrative. Her interest was only to keep me talking.

"We returned home and after Christmas, went to Glasgow. We were to be the guests of honor at an educational institute. I suffered an early miscarriage on the train. I did not attend the programme but I know Charles met with tremendous success. The crowds could not have enough of him. Charles wanted to do some more travelling but the doctors insisted we return so that I could rest. I took to bed immediately and it took me almost a month to recover. I spent just a few weeks on my feet before I was sick again; I was pregnant with Henry. That was also a difficult birth. The baby was positioned awkwardly. Charles decided we would use chloroform. The chloroform made the birth easier as the baby could be turned without me feeling pain. But I felt it harmed me in some way; I recovered physically but I started nervous headaches. Charles wouldn't hear of it. He said it was my imagination, soon all the doctors would be using chloroform."

"Kate, since my earliest memories, I remember you as being pregnant or recovering from childbirth or miscarriage."

"Is that not the lot of most women? Mama, my mother-in-law, most of our aunts and cousins have eight to ten children and who knows how many miscarriages. As women we have to go through this cycle of repeated births, lose our health and looks, and if we are lucky, gain the regard of our families, otherwise be cast aside."

"Kate, I'm sorry, I did not mean to upset you. I never had these thoughts before but I feel now you may have been better without ..."

"No, don't say it, Helen. I don't regret any of the pain, and least of all I regret the next pregnancy, a few months after Henry's birth. It gave me Dora. She was a beautiful baby. Charles was delighted. He always wanted daughters; I think he saw them as a lesser responsibility.

122

Dora was born on 15th August of 1850 and left us on 14th of April the following year, but she lives in my heart."

"As she lives in all our hearts," Helen said, taking my hand.

"Charles had started *Household Words* the previous year and it kept him very busy. Charley was at Eton; he went the same year Dora was born. Another important change was, we moved to Tavistock House. Charles had been looking for a bigger house, to comfortably accommodate us all, as he did not want to move again. He spent a lot of money and time in getting Tavistock House ready. We were all excited about the move."

"You did a lot of entertaining in those days. I was too young to attend but I heard the details with great interest."

"Yes, since moving to Devonshire Terrace, we hosted many lavish dinners. Charles had become a well-known figure. He was friends with many interesting people, including the prime minister.

"The years passed by quickly. Charles wrote his novels, edited the newspaper, entertained, we made family trips, the children grew, left home for the boarding house Charles had found suitable. Helen, you wanted me to speak of happy times. Those were happy times, when nothing unexpected happened. I might have sometimes thought those days dull, when I lay in confinement with a baby on the way, and the rest of the household went about their regular days. But dullness, and a regular day, with the small arguments and annoyances, the smiles, the petty squabbles even, summed together to form happiness."

"You did not mention Plorn's birth."

"Edward, nicknamed the Noble Plorn, was a little of a surprise. Charles had recently become interested in avoiding...learning means of..."

"You can't put me to blush, I'm an old maid. Charles was doing something to prevent more children, right?"

"Yes, that is why Plorn was unexpected but not unwelcome. As no more children followed to sap my energy, I devoted more time to Plorn than I had done to my other children. I fear I spoilt him."

"All of us did. Mama misses his dreadfully. Charles has put us in a difficult situation. This separation need not have been so painful. He has turned it into a bitter quarrel. The children are not to speak to Mama or me, or to Mark Lemon. Our friends are not to invite me; he calls me a serpent and forces everyone to take sides. It is cruel to separate children from their mother, and relations."

What could I say? I knew my mother considered the day as blighted when Charles first came to our home. Quite unreasonably, she blamed my father for befriending him and bringing him home, as if he had some means of seeing the future. But then, grief is never reasonable and my mother had enough to grieve about.

Her grief was in fact greater than mine. One daughter buried, two shamed, and Helen, not married and most likely ruined by the scandal surrounding Georgy and me. She loved her grandchildren, and she worried about them, and longed for them. She aged visibly in a very short time. I was very careful to hide my true feelings in front of her. I knew for her sake, and for my father's sake, I had to be strong.

Her weakened state, and Helen's strength, kept me moving from day to day, and from breaking down, so that I faced visitors with a degree of composure.

We had many visitors in the first few months. Some were friends, who came in genuine sympathy, some came out of curiosity, and others for sniffing out a scandal.

At first I met them with Helen by my side, but after a few months, I was receiving them by myself. I had never made scintillating conversation, neither did I now. But I learnt to parry the cruel thrusts some of my guests made.

I took care to announce my presence before entering a room by speaking loudly to my maid, to save my visitors and myself from embarrassment. But sometimes I stopped noiselessly and listened.

"Do you think she feels anything? She looks so calm," one would say.

"But not unstable, I think. Of course, one can never be sure about such things. Her husband must have had a reason," another would answer.

"Poor man, it must have been a terrible ordeal for him. He is brilliant, and veritably dazzles in any company. I always thought Mrs. Dickens was not spirited enough for him," another caller would commiserate with Charles.

Sometimes a caller would express her sympathy for me. "No, I don't think there's anything the matter with Mrs. Dickens. I've always found her pleasing and gentle mannered."

I started receiving invitations, again for the same reasons; some were out of friendship, the others were to satisfy curiosity.

As I was not up to visiting socially, I declined most of them. The ones I accepted were from friends and relatives, and I accepted them to please Mama and Helen.

Perhaps, as the years passed, everyone would learn to accept my unhappy situation but at that time, my presence was a strain on the company present. They tried to touch on topics that did not include Charles, which was extremely difficult because Charles' books and serials *were* the topic of drawing room conversation everywhere. I decided, the next time I was in company, I would initiate a discussion myself.

Charles was writing *A Tale of Two Cities*. He had left *Household Words*; he quarreled with the publishers, Bradbury and Evans who also owned *Punch*, as they had refused to publish his notice about his domestic situation in their paper. Charles thought they were siding with me, though their reasons for not publishing the notice were their own. Charles left their paper and started his own newspaper, *All the Year Round*. *A Tale of Two Cities* was his first serialized fiction in this paper.

I read each episode and knew they were quite popular. The next time I dined at Mark Lemon's, whom Charles now treated as an enemy, I spoke the words I had rehearsed. I said, "My husband's new fiction is shaping very well, I think. I find myself eagerly anticipating the next weekly episode."

My words were received by shocked silence. Mark was looking at me, slack jawed. He had acted for me in the separation and knew the extent of my heartbreak.

One guest made a comment about the character, Sydney Carton, and the others joined in. I slowly placed my cup on a table. My hand was trembling noticeably and I was afraid I would drop it.

FIFTEEN

Empty - In and Out

I sat for long spells without thinking, without feeling, like an object suspended in time. Or maybe I was taken out of time and I watched its passage, disinterested, as it went past without touching me. My days were a succession of seconds, minutes, and hours; I neither anticipated them nor regretted their passing.

When I thought, it was of my children. They all seemed far away. In truth, they were far away. Walter continued to be in India. He was not bearing up against the hostile weather; however, he had received a promotion and was a lieutenant. Sydney was on a ship; he was fourteen and a navy cadet. He had come home, his home, not mine, before joining the ship. How I had longed to spend time with him!

Charley had left for Honkong on a tea buying trip; he was venturing into business.

This was 1860, two years since I was branded useless and discarded. Kate was married; she married Charles Collins on July 17. I did not know her reasons for the marriage as Charles was much older to her. He was thirty-two to her twenty, and almost an invalid. Charley suspected she wanted to get away from the situation at home which she was finding intolerable. I hoped it was not true; even marrying for love could turn out unhappily but marrying for the wrong reasons would surely be disastrous.

Kate's wedding was a grand one. It was at the country home at Gad's Hill. Charles had arranged for a special train to bring the guests from London. The wedding was like a pastoral festival, I read, with people from the village strewing flowers in the churchyard and erecting triumphal arches, and firing guns as a happy salute.

I spent the week before the wedding in a state of nerves; for a while I would be certain that Kate would insist on having me by her side. I feverishly worked on a veil for Kate, and looked over my gowns, and refurbished one too, after which I decided I should get a new one. I also spend anxious hours, certain I would not be called, only to take heart again that my presence would be quite acceptable, in fact it would be expected.

But I was not invited. Perhaps, if Charley was in London, I would have made him take me to Gad's Hill. Perhaps.

My daughter was married without me to bless her. I told myself it did not matter, she had my blessings come what may, but it did matter, it did hurt. It was a priceless moment and it was gone, never to be reclaimed.

With Charley away, I lapsed into a despondent state. I brooded about Kate and her reasons for getting married. Charles Collins was Wilkie Collin's brother. I had heard that Wilkie Collins was living with a woman in sin, and doing it openly. I remembered someone had once suggested Charles had broken his marriage because he saw Wilkie living happily with Caroline Graves, without the constraints and responsibility of marriage. Now Kate was a part of that family.

Helen was often busy with her singing students and could not visit very often. I neither had anything to do nor was I inclined towards industry. Everywhere in the city, mothers and wives were living the way I once did, centered around their home and children. Some were too poor to have help, and did all the heavy work themselves; others planned the work and supervised the servants. Did they realize their fortune?

Women are brought up with the aim of marriage and raising their own families. I was. I did not contemplate another existence and now did not know what I should do. Charles was satisfied he has dealt fairly with me. He had settled an annuity on me and set me up in a house. He was not wrong. He could have left me penniless and I would not have been able to do a thing. He has only hinted at my 'mental disturbance'; he could have declared me a lunatic and got me locked away. I was his wife, his chattel by law.

Charles provided me with the means to live, but what was I to do with this life? I was alone and terribly lonely. I would have managed my situation differently if, like Charles or other men, I had something to occupy my hands and head.

I saw from the papers that Charles was busy with his work. Before our separation, he had commenced public reading from his novels, and he was continuing it. I followed his triumphs. The public adored him, they laughed and wept with him, they chanted his name. I could imagine the scene; I had been witness to people, ordinary people, who were moved to tears by shaking his hand, the hand that wrote about Domby, and Little Nell.

My small house was not very far from my former home. My servants, who watched me in sympathetic silence, sometimes brought me news from Tavistock House. They had some family connection with the servants there. I did not discourage them but listened in grateful silence.

They told me that Mamie graced the table, she tried to give instructions to the servants, though she deferred in everything to her aunt. They told me Charles wrote regularly from wherever he was travelling for his public readings; the letters were sometimes read aloud for the benefit of Plorn, and the servants overheard. They reported Charles was getting very tired after the readings and the hectic travelling; he had terrible colds, and his secretary, Arthur, was ill. They told me when he was present in London and when he left, and I accepted these crumbs from them gratefully and often pressed a shilling into their hands.

Many times, I thought I would take advantage of Charles' absence and visit my former home but Georgy would be there, and I did not put it beyond her to bar my entry.

Whenever Charles and the family moved to Gad's Hill, which was quite often, I turned to Charley for news as he communicated with his sisters.

One day Charley brought me news that saddened me. Charles was selling Tavistock House. With Kate married and the boys, all except Plorn, away from home, he did not want such a big house in London. The family would move permanently to Gad's Hill. For himself, he had furnished rooms in his office and if the rest of them wanted to spend a season in London, he would rent a house.

I remembered the joy and the happiness with which Charles had leased Tavistock House for fifty years; for our lifetime, he had told me. He had lavished much care on the repairs and the modifications and not spared any expense in furnishing the house. Though my memory of Tavistock House was tarnished because it was linked to the collapse of my marriage, it also represented hope. I wished that the turbulence between us would be settled; I wished Charles would come to his senses, and we would live in this dream mansion, and grow old in it, with our children and grandchildren.

The sale made me wonder. Charles had carried out the separation with such haste that it was obvious to everyone he could not wait to get rid of me. His subsequent behavior indicated he was only too happy to live without me. Friends reported he was as witty and humorous in company as ever. But did the house hold memories for him, too? Did they bother him? Make him remorseful? Was that why he was selling it?

Charley cut my fancies short. He hinted Charles had sold the house to economise. He was maintaining Ellen, her sisters and mother in style. He had purchased a four-storied terraced house with a garden for Ellen in a good section of London. He did not mind selling Tavistock House to lavish money on them. What he found burdensome, and complained to a friend about, was the annuity he was forced to pay to 'his Angel Wife'.

So much for my dreams! How easily, and foolishly, I was swayed by my heart! Why could I not accept, irrevocably, that Charles did not want me in his life? He was quite happy will his present dalliance.

Why indeed? Because I believed in him. For all the times he had hurt me, he had been a good and loving husband a hundred times over. I loved him, I believed he was essentially good, I respected him, I admired him, I thought he was a man of lofty principles, sadly gone astray.

There was someone else who thought like me. Miss Coutts, dear friend and well-wisher, wrote to Charles again, and tried to end our estrangement.

She explained to me, "It is not just for you and your children's sake, but for his, too. He looks tired and unhappy. He has turned bitter and has cut himself off from people who are genuinely his friends."

Her observations were correct. Charley told me his father looked tired and ill. I knew Charles was travelling a lot and public readings were more strenuous than writing, but Charles was not like other people. He loved travelling; the hustle and bustle did not bother him. The malaise was more probably due to leading a life of secrets. Charley told me that very few people knew about Ellen and they all kept it a secret. With an understanding born of our years together, I knew such an arrangement would be distasteful to Charles. Poor Charles, he could not divorce me, and I was nowhere close to dying!

Charles refused Miss Coutts' counsel. He was adamant. He would not reconcile.

His refusal filled me with rage. Could he not see what harm this separation was doing to our children? He made it sound as if everything was well by saying Georgina and Mamie kept house and the children were all in agreement of the arrangement. How could they be? How could any child be? He would not know. He never knew what the children wanted. He called me an indifferent mother but in truth, he was the indifferent one. Sometimes I wondered whether he even knew their names in proper order. He liked to boast about them as exceptional to his friends, exceptional because they were his children, weren't they, but he never cared much about them.

Walter had wanted to become a writer. He liked writing and wanted to follow in his father's path. Charles decided against it. Walter would not be happy as a writer, he decided, and sent him away on a long voyage to India, at a time when other parents were thinking of bringing back their sons because of the Sepoy Mutiny. Walter had been sixteen and not interested in becoming a soldier.

Charley was doing well at Eton but Charles pulled him out when he was sixteen and told him to decide upon a career. Charley was keen on becoming an army officer, and Miss Coutts, his godmother, would have bought him a commission, but Charles had other ideas. He decided Charley should go into commerce. He sent him to Germany to learn commercial skills. Charley learnt German but his teacher informed Charles that Charley had no bent for commerce. Charles tried placing him with other mentors and finally, Charley took up a position in Barings Bank. Kate was interested in acting but Charles often discouraged her.

Now, when cancer has claimed me and I'm waiting to die, I've a glimmer of understanding about why Charles tore up our lives. But then, and for many years thereafter, I often wrestled with the question: why?

One such night, when I was unable to sleep, I pulled out the trunk at the bottom of which I had stored Charles' letters. The smaller packet contained his letters to me during our courtship. I fingered the ribbon and the love knot but did not open it.

Keeping it aside, I opened the bundle of letters he wrote to me after we were wed. I had found the letters loving and affectionate, filled with news he wanted to share, and his enquiries about my welfare and that of our children. Had I missed something in them? Did they have hidden in them the secret to his change of heart?

I read the precious words, nay, I heard them in Charles' voice. *My darling Kate, My dear Kate, My dearest Catherine*..all the letters commenced with such fond addresses.

I smoothed open an old letter. Charles had written it two and a half years after our wedding.

Lion Hotel, Shrewsbury, Thursday, Nov. 1st, 1838.

My dearest Love,

I received your welcome letter on arriving here last night, and am rejoiced to hear that the dear children are so much better. I hope that in your next, or your next but one, I shall learn that they are quite well. A thousand kisses to them. I wish I could convey them myself.

God bless you, my darling. I long to be back with you again and to see the sweet Babs.

136

Your faithful and most affectionate Husband

I read the next letter, and the next, reliving my days as a cherished wife and mother.

I wished I could show them to everyone who mocked me, or pitied me. If Charles was unhappy, miserable, as he had alleged, why did he write by every post, filling sheets of paper with his news? I wanted to show the letters, not only from our early days of wedded bliss, but also of later years.

Piazza Coffee House, Covent Garden,
Monday, Dec. 2nd, 1844.
My dearest Kate,

I received, with great delight, your excellent letter of this morning. Do not regard this as my answer to it.[133] It is merely to say that I've been at Bradbury and Evans's all day, and have barely time to write more than that I will write to-morrow.....

He said he was pressed for time, and yet the letter described his meeting with his friends and how they received his book, 'The Chimes'. Did that not prove we were very much close and he shared his life with me? This was eight years after we were married.

I picked up another long letter, which begun with

58, Lincoln's Inn Fields, Saturday, Dec. 19th, 1846.
My dearest Kate,

I really am bothered to death by this confounded dramatization of the Christmas book. They were in a state so horrible at Keeley's yesterday (as perhaps Forster told you when he wrote), that I was obliged to engage to read the book to them this morning.

It described, in great detail, some problems he was having, after which he shared his success: *Christmas book published to-day—twenty-three thousand copies already gone!!! Browne's plates for next "Dombey" much better than usual......*

All the letters were the same, filled with news and his desire to share his life with me.

I concentrated on the later years but did not find any change in their tenor.

Rome, Monday, Nov. 14th, 1853.

My dearest Catherine,

As I've mentioned in my letter to Georgy (written last night but posted with this), I received her letter without yours, to my unbounded astonishment. This morning, on sending again to the post-office, I at last got yours, and most welcome it is with all its contents.........

This was five years before our separation.

2, Rue St. Florentin, Tuesday, Oct. 16th, 1855.

My dearest Catherine,

We have had the most awful job to find a place that would in the least suit us, for Paris is perfectly full, and there is nothing to be got at any sane price......

This was three years before our separation.

Tavistock House, Monday, May 5th, 1856.

My dear Catherine,

I did nothing at Dover (except for "Household Words"), and have not begun "Little Dorrit," No. 8, yet. But I took twenty-mile walks in the fresh air, and perhaps in the long run did better than if I had been at work. The report concerning Scheffer's portrait I had from Ward. It[434] is in the best place in the largest room, but I find the general impression of the artists exactly mine. They almost all say that it wants something; that nobody could mistake whom it was meant for, but that it has something disappointing in it, etc. etc. Stanfield likes it better than any of the other painters, I think. His own picture is magnificent. And Frith, in a "Little Child's Birthday Party," is quite delightful. There are many interesting pictures. When you see Scheffer, tell him from me that Eastlake, in his speech at the dinner, referred to the portrait as "a contribution from a distinguished man of genius in France, worthy of himself and of his subject."

Charles wrote this two years before he insisted I was not suited to be his wife. It was a long letter in which he shared his impressions about many things.

The letters that followed were similar, until our trip to Manchester, after which he did not write. I spent the night reading scores of letters, yet I remained clueless. I replaced the letters in the trunk, not before kissing them, and opened the newspaper which had Charles' letter of two years ago.

London, W. E., Tavistock House, Tavistock Square, Tuesday^ Twenty-fifth May, 1858. To Arthur Smith, Esq. :—

Mrs. Dickens and I've lived unhappily together for many years. Hardly any one who has known us intimately can fail to have known that we are, in all respects of character and temperament, wonderfully unsuited to each other. *I suppose that no two people, not vicious in themselves, ever were joined together who had a greater difficulty in understanding one another, or who had less in common.*

Nothing has, on many occasions, stood between us and a separation but Mrs. Dickens's sister, Georgina Hogarth. *From the age of fifteen she has devoted herself to our house and our children. She has been their playmate, nurse, instructress, friend, protectress, adviser, companion.* In the manly consideration towards Mrs. Dickens which I owe to my wife, I will only remark of her that the peculiarity of her character has thrown all the children on someone else. *I do not know—I can't by any stretch of fancy imagine—what would have become of them but for this aunt, who has grown up with them, to whom they are devoted, and who has sacrificed the best part of her youth and life to them.*

She has remonstrated, reasoned, suffered and toiled, and came again to prevent a separation between Mrs. Dickens and me. Mrs. Dickens has often expressed to her, her sense of her affectionate care and devotion in the house— never more strongly than within the last twelve months.

For some years past Mrs. Dickens has been in the habit of representing to me that it would be better for her to go away and live apart; that _her always increasing estrangement was due to a mental disorder under which she sometimes labors; more, that she felt herself unfit for the life she had to lead, as my wife, and that she would be better far away._ I've uniformly replied that she must bear our misfortune, and fight the fight out to the end; that the children were the first consideration ; and that I feared they must bind us together in " appearance."

At length, within these three weeks, it was suggested to me by Forster that, even for their sakes, it would surely be better to construct and rearrange their unhappy home. I empowered him to treat with Mrs. Dickens, as the friend of both of us for one and twenty years. Mrs. Dickens wished to add, on her part, Mark Lemon, and did so. On Saturday last Lemon wrote to Forster that Mrs. Dickens " gratefully and thankfully accepted " the terms I proposed to her. Of the pecuniary part of them I will only say that I believe they are as generous as if Mrs. Dickens were a lady of distinction, and I a man of fortune. The remaining parts of them are easily described—my eldest boy to live with Mrs. Dickens and to take care of her; my eldest girl to keep my house, *both my girls and all my children, but the eldest son, to live with me in the continued companionship of their Aunt Georgina, for whom they have all the tenderest affection that I've ever seen among young people, and who has a higher claim (as I've often declared, for many years), upon my affection, respect and gratitude than anybody in this world.*

I hope that no one who may become acquainted with what I write here, can possibly be so cruel and unjust as to put any misconstruction on our separation, so far. My elder children all understand it perfectly, and all accept it as inevitable.

There is not a shadow of doubt or concealment among us. My eldest son and I are one as to it all.

Two wicked persons, who should have spoken very differently of me, in consideration of earnest respect and gratitude, have (as I am told, and, indeed, to my personal knowledge) coupled with this separation the name of a young lady for whom I've a great attachment and regard. I will not repeat her name—I honor it too much. Upon my soul and honor, there is not on this earth a more virtuous and spotless creature than that young lady. I know her to be innocent and pure, and as good as my own dear daughters.

Further, I am quite sure that Mrs. Dickens, having received this assurance from me, must now believe it in the respect I know her to have for me, and in the perfect confidence I know her in her better moments to repose in my truthfulness.

On this head, again, there is not a shadow of doubt or concealment between my children and me. All is open and plain among us, as though we were brothers and sisters. They are perfectly certain that I would not deceive them, and the confidence among us is without a fear. C. D.

I knew each word of the dastardly letter, yet I read it again, and contrasted it with his letters of before. They were like letters written by two different people.

When Charles picked up his powerful pen to malign me, and to deny our life together with well-constructed lies, he knew I would not expose him. I would not take his letters to the press, or give interviews, or write letters to editors. He knew me well, my husband, and also knew how to rid himself of me.

What was the sum total of my life? Married at twenty-one, made a virtual widow at forty-three, gave birth ten times and miscarried thrice in sixteen years, I was like a prisoner in goal. Alone, away from the people I loved the most, my exile was complete. If only I knew my crime!

As the emptiness suffocated me, I wondered about Ellen Ternan. Charley had confessed she lived not very far from my house. What did she do the whole day? How did she spend her time when Charles was away? Did she have a baby? Did she realize Charles was capable of snatching it away?

SIXTEEN

Orphan in Death

After concluding business at Hongkong, Charley travelled to India and spent some time with Walter. Walter had been made lieutenant.

"Is he content?" I asked, still remembering his tearful face of three years ago.

"He is reconciled, he knows there is nothing else for him to do."

"Does the weather agree with him?"

Charley said, slowly, with a worried frown, "The truth is he did not look good. He's in the infantry and often suffers from bad health. He is also living beyond his means."

"I fear it is not the life for him. He is only twenty. He can still choose another career. Why don't you speak to your father?" I said impulsively.

"You know why! He counts the expense of each son but squanders money on that..."

"Shsh..Charley!" I laid a hand on his arm. Charley was usually cool tempered, which was another point that hankered with Charles. He complained the boys got their lassitude from me. He never realized the boys did not show any spirit because he always cut them down, not by harsh words but by mockery and witticisms at their expense.

"Charley, you will have to speak to your father about Bessie," I reminded. Bessie was the daughter of Frederick Evans, one time publisher and friend of Charles, now an enemy because like many of our friends, Evans did not support Charles when he forced a separation on false pretences.

Charley and Bessie were childhood sweethearts. Everyone, including Charles, was aware of this fact. I feared Charles would want Charley to disassociate himself from Bessie, as a show of loyalty to him. Charley would again be compelled to take a stand against his father and this time it could lead to a complete breach between them.

When Charley informed his father he would like to take Bessie for his wife, Charles exploded in anger, and characteristically blamed me. "Your foolish mother has put you up to this," he accused.

Charley could not get his father's blessings to the match. It was a blow to him. Charles had been a larger than life figure for him and the other children. They strived to please him, and his approval was the reward they looked forward to. What Charley had done for me was truly admirable and now he was defying Charles again and marrying Bessie. He was also entering into partnership with Bessie's brother.

Charles did not attend the wedding; he kept himself engaged touring Scotland. He tried to stop his friends from attending and spoke ill of Bessie. The poor child was bewildered; she had known Charles for many years and was shocked by the way he slandered her. I think that is when she fully understood the extent of canards he had spread against me.

I was delighted with the wedding. Charley was marrying the woman he loved and for myself, I was getting a daughter. A year later, the happy couple was blessed with a baby girl, and when I held her in my arms, for the first time in four years I forgot my sorrows.

I spent a lot of time with my son's family. I busied myself with knitting and stitching for the baby. I recollected old recipes. Helen and Mama were happy. Helen told me, "Kate, you are finally looking the way you were before. You are now my sweet Kate again and I've Bessie to thank for it!"

Helen was right. I felt the change myself. I was taking interest in the world around me. I was not following Charles in the newspapers as before and I looked to Charley for latest news about the baby, not about my daughters or Plorn.

I still missed my children and remembered them but I had finally accepted I had no place in their lives. I was only a distant presence, whom they may or may not recall.

My father was a respected music critic and a musicologist. He had authored several books on music and contributed scholarly articles to newspapers and journals. My mother also loved music and we played music, not for money or fame, but for the love of it.

Helen was quite different from most other young women; she was certainly different from her sisters and cousins. She was passionate about making a career in music. She was a vocalist; she performed and also taught singing. Her friends were mostly musicians. Since my changed circumstances, she wanted me to join in their gatherings. I reluctantly went a few times for her sake. Now I was willingly accompanying her and joining in the informal sessions. I started making new friends and found a measure of happiness.

My mother said one day, "Kate, I fear if I die, I will not be buried with dear Mary. Your husband will not allow it."

"Why do you think of such sad events when you have many more years to live?"

However, as it sometimes happens, my mother's words turned out to be a premonition of her death. She died in August 1863, spending the last five years of her life worrying about her daughters and longing for her grandchildren.

I wrote to Charles for the first time since our separation, asking him about the funeral arrangements. He had acquired the burial plot for Mary. It also held the remains of my brother, who had died a couple of years after Mary. At that time, Charles had unwillingly permitted him to be buried in the same grave; he had this wish to be himself buried with Mary.

Charles did not immediately reply but he did pass on the necessary instructions and we had the satisfaction of fulfilling my mother's wishes.

I was not surprised that Charles did not send me condolences for my mother's death, something a mere acquaintance would have done. He was hard and implacable, an enemy in life and in death.

Helen and I, my brothers and father grieved for my mother and in this sad hour, we sent word to Georgina but she did not come. Even the death of her own mother was not sufficient to break her misplaced loyalty to Charles. On the day of the funeral, she was playing hostess to the De la Rues in Gad's Hill.

Charley was of course there; he had always been a loving grandson. My other children were absent, which was not unexpected but sad, given the love and affection my mother had lavished on them.

My mother's death was a forerunner to a tragedy infinitely greater, for the death of one's child is much more painful than the death of an aged parent.

On 7th February, 1864, which was Charles' birthday, he received news that Walter had died suddenly in Calcutta, on the last night of the year of 1863. He was only twenty-three. Walter, poor Walter, who had loved his studies and liked nothing better than to read and write, died in a distant foreign land, possibly uncared for, without any dear one to mourn him.

The news put me in a frenzy of grief. I had seen Walter before this hateful separation, and had hoped to see him again soon. Charley had told me Walter was coming home on sick leave; he was sure he would come to see me. But now never! I wanted to rage at Charles for sending him away, I wanted to weep with Charles for the untimely death of our child, I wanted to hold my living children in my arms and feel Walter's presence in their warm bodies.

But, even the death of our young son did not move Charles. He neither came to see me nor sent for me. He did not even send a letter to say that he grieved for the child, though he had not been happy about his conception.

Charley consoled me, as did Bessie, and Helen and my darling granddaughter by her sweet innocence presence but I yearned for Charles, the father of my child, the man I had loved without reserve.

Poor Miss Coutts! She thought that the death would bring the grieving parents together; she tried again but failed. I know she was shocked that Charles could be this hard, as I would have been shocked six years ago, but I knew better now.

Did he even mourn this child or were his tears reserved for the characters in his book? He had wept for Little Dora after he had killed off the character.

I doubt he shed a tear for Walter. Charley told me later that Walter had got into debt in India, and Charles had been angry with him. He had not replied to his letters even when he knew of the illness. No, Charles would have judged him and found him wanting, and shut his heart against him.

SEVENTEEN

Loved, Never Honoured

A change came over me after Walter's death. This was a bigger wound, bigger than my separation, and it turned my heart away from Charles. I no longer made excuses for him, or tried to see the good in him and explain away the evil as the necessary aberration of genius.

Until then, I had tried to find reasons for Charles' behavior but I could not condone his cold-hearted conduct when Walter died. Some friends who called upon me remarked that Charles was bearing up well, very well indeed. No one saw him shed a tear, or postpone his engagements, or mourn Walter in any way. What kind of a father did not mourn his own flesh and blood? The kind that tore away his children from their mother, naturally. When I remembered Charles' grief at Mary's death, or even at the death of some of our friends, I could only conclude that whatever affection Charles once had for the children was dead. He did not care for them. He cared only for his own pleasure, and for Ellen.

I worried about my boys more than ever before. I could not see them, so I wrote to them, and tried to keep my letters as normal as possible, as if we were still a united family.

I saw little of them but when I did, we met almost as strangers, or rather with strangeness. The meetings never went well. My sons could not let me into their feelings, their fears, for they had forgotten what it was to have a mother, and to confide in her. For my part, I was anxious about them, as Charles was sending them off to the corners of the earth, as if England held no opportunities for young men, and though I saw the fear and uncertainty in their eyes, I could not speak about it.

Thus, on the very rare occasions that I saw my children, I marveled at how much they had grown, and how well they looked, but I did not ask, "Son, are you happy? And content with what your father has planned for you?"

I failed them, as surely as their father, and in the coming years, watched my sons stumble, and fall, and flounder, in the manner of a rudderless vessel at sea.

Poor, unfortunate boys, born to an unfortunate mother! Unwanted by their father since conception, torn asunder from their mother, foisted on an aunt who did not know what to do with them, and finally blamed by their father that they were not at all what he expected them to be.

Charles often compared them to himself. He had made a great success of his life, he told them, he had succeeded against great odds and without their advantages. Charles did not grasp the essential difference. He had grown up with the knowledge that he *had* to make his own way, he *had* to earn his living because his father could not or did not. He was prepared.

But for his sons, to see their father make a lot of money, yet send them away to lead lives they were not equipped for, was painful. A father who made much of them when they were boys, but thrust them out to become sheep farmers, and soldiers, as soon as they turned sixteen, was bewildering. Added to this was their belief that they were not worth much; had they not inherited traits from their foolish mother?

My sons went far out into the world but did not have the simple protection of self-confidence, and the knowledge that they were complete persons, and loved.

"Why do they have to go? They can start as clerks in London, and find their own way. Life in the Colonies is harsh, and we have already lost Walter," I told Charley, though I knew Charles would not heed anyone.

"He is ashamed of us all," Charley told me bitterly. "He complains about his sons to his friends, and tells them that they astound him by their incompetence."

I thought Charles had too many secrets, and that was why he did not want his sons in London. He exiled them, as he exiled me, for his own sake, and blamed us all.

My friends did not see any change in me in my altered circumstances. They did not hear me condemn Charles, or protest about him. I continued as before, and listened politely when anyone spoke about Charles, and discussed his books.

Within a year of my separation, my friends and acquaintances believed I was reconciled to my situation and had accepted it with dignity. Some even went so far as to praise my behavior of Christian forbearance.

They would have been surprised to learn I owed my composure to the years I had spent with Charles, for it was in my marriage I learnt to hide my real feelings.

I had learnt, at all times, to remain self-possessed. Charles was very changeable. He would be sweet and loving, and suddenly he would make a cruel jest at my expense. This was especially when we had company. In the early days, I would leave the room and lapse into easy tears, and reproach him when he sought me out.

"What did I say?" he would ask, surprised. "Why did you take offence, after all it was only with Forster I spoke thus, and Kate, you must agree your taste in literature is abysmal."

He was a good mimic, as was Georgy. They were not above joining forces and imitating me, making the children roar with laughter and the servants smile. I had learnt it was better to hold on to an amiable expression than to protest. My family and our friends thought I was game for anything because I joined in the laughter against me. Charles, and I think a few others, construed I was too dull to realize that he sharpened his wit at my expense.

None knew that my amiability was my shield, my defense. By smiling away the moment, I drew less attention to it. No one knew I often dreaded the times when Charles swung to his moods of excessive jollity, for it was then he was at his cruelest.

I hid my distress well but on rare occasions, a guest would notice. Hans Anderson was one such guest. When he visited Gad's Hill, after an enjoyable dinner and Charles' famous punch, Charles said something uncomplimentary about me. It was one of his favorite jokes, and it showed me as clumsy and slow. Georgy took it up from there. She mimicked me, or rather caricatured me. Everyone laughed, so did I.

Hans caught my eye. He looked uncomfortable, and there was such sympathy and understanding in his eyes that I felt sudden tears threatening to reveal my hurt. I quickly left the room and returned ten minutes later, with a glib reason for my absence.

With so much practice behind me, it was easy to maintain the same façade in my changed circumstances. Friends were surprised, then reassured, that I was coping well, and not much changed by my misfortune. They did not know I was shattered into a million pieces by my husband's mindless cruelty, they could not guess I was wounded and suffered untold agonies for my children.

My children. They were another reason for my apparent calm. I was resolved never to lay upon them the burden of my sorrows. They had enough to bear on their own. Even Charley had come to believe I had accept my sad state. I had not. I had only stopped hoping, I had not stopped longing.

EIGHTEEN

Widow of Charles Dickens

It is twelve years of my virtual widowhood. The early years were spent in a fog of bafflement and disbelief. What had happened to me? How? Why? Could someone help? Would someone help?

I was scared and terrified of the future. My life was over at forty-three and I had to live on. My entire being longed for the comforting presence of children, home, and yes, a husband, whose presence I had got used to. But time had smoothed away my fears and absorbed the worst of my pain.

I asked myself all sorts of questions. I asked what if it was love, the kind that moved mountains? Perhaps, Charles and Ellen loved each other that way, and I had come in the way of their union. Was that why he looked so beaten, and tired and old? Was this love so great that it made him forget his duties as a father, and a husband? Was it love, and not the lust we all thought it was.

Who would know? But even if it was love, did he have the right to separate me from my children, and my children from a stable home, and blacken my name? Why did he and Ellen not wait to be united in the other world, like the characters of *Hard Times?*

Why blame me? Why not announce his love, and live with Ellen, society be damned? Other men had done it. But no. Charles was a selfish man, a weak man, who thought only of himself, his image, his popularity. He did not bother to count the hurts he caused, the hearts he lacerated.

He was selfish, and weak, yet he believed himself strong, and incorruptible.

After he left me, I made new bonds, and these were the ones I could depend upon, for they had been forged in adversity. Helen and I remained close even after she was married. I loved her daughter May, and she held me in great affection.

I discovered freedom away from Charles. I learnt to breathe freely, to move without fear of criticism, to talk and laugh without the thought that Charles would find my friends or my behavior wanting. I could read whatever I wanted, and have my own opinions, and not worry that Charles would call them pretentious or mock me to his friends. These were small things, but precious.

I accepted, finally, I had no place in Charles' life, and instead of beating my wings like a trapped moth and hurting myself, I learnt to use my status as his wife like an armour. I treated myself, and was treated by others, as Mrs. Charles Dickens.

I read all episodes of *The Tales of Two cites*, *Great Expectations*, and *Our Mutual friend*. I privately thought the joy had gone out of his writing. The comic characters, the innocence, was missing. The craft was superior, but the soul had left. However, I kept these impressions to myself.

If anyone asked questions about Charles' work, I answered them and people thought I was on cordial terms with him. His dramatic readings from his books were reported in the newspapers. They were a rage with the public; people were laughing and crying as he held centre stage. My friends and acquaintances spoke to me about the readings, and I did not let on that I had not seen them. I did not even tell them that Charles, in the early years of our marriage, read out the very same part to me, the murder of Nancy, from Oliver Twist. He was so menacing and evil that I had become frightened. I had told him, to his great satisfaction, that he was not acting out an evil part, he *was* evil.

He made a similarly strong impact when he read from his Christmas story, *The Chimes*, and had his friends in tears. He was thrilled to have such power. He must be ecstatic now, with the public response he was getting.

These were private recollections and I did not share them. Instead I politely agreed that yes, Charles was hypnotic, mesmerizing, and capable of making his audience believe whatever story he told them.

Charles was in a train accident in 1865. Like thousands of other people I sent him a letter of enquiry. Later he went to America on a reading tour; I sent him good wishes. His replies were in the manner he would have replied to countless other people; probably his replies were more curt to me than to them.

He was very successful, and Charley, who was now reconciled with his father, and worked as his subeditor, told me he was not keeping well. The dramatic readings and the frequent travelling was taxing his health. His doctors suspected he may have suffered a stroke. A few months later, Charley told me his father was at Gad's Hill, and better. He had decided to give up the public readings but would have one last farewell round.

I listened to Charley's bits of news and felt a little more than polite interest. I had signed a document twelve years ago affirming separation by mutual consent, but it had taken me that many years to feel separated.

Charley rushed to Gad's Hill on June 9, 1870. He had received the distressing news that his father was very ill. The next morning Kate came up from Gad's Hill to see me, and to tell me that Charles had expired the previous evening. I was now his widow in thought and deed.

After giving me the news, Kate suddenly fell into my arms in a paroxysm of tears. I held her, wiped her face with my handkerchief, patted her, and gave her tea, but I did not shed a tear.

"I'll be ready in a few minutes," I told her.

"Mama, Georgy told me to tell you that your presence ..."

"Is not welcome? Is that why you came? Were you all terrified I would rush down at the news of death?" I asked bitterly.

Kate looked away and I regretted my harsh words. She was a victim, as were all my children, a victim of an arrogant man who was now beyond any reproach.

After Kate left, I told the maid I would not be receiving anyone, and shut myself in my room.

I lay down on my bed and stared at the ceiling. It was a bright day and sunshine splashed into my room. I went to the window and drew the heavy curtains close. Much, much better!

The room was dark, and it matched my deepening gloom. How had I convinced myself that I was separate from Charles? *He* had cut himself off; if it was me lying dead, he would be probably planning a respectful marriage to Ellen but I was not indifferent to him.

Proof was in my silent screams. Charles dead! My husband was no more; he was dead and with him had died all my hopes of reconciliation. I would never be a cherished wife again. The wrongs done against me would never be righted in this world. I would never be able to tell him that in many ways I still loved him.

Loved him? No, I hated him for viciously cutting me off from his life and our family, as if I were a gangrenous limb, threatening to poison everyone by my presence. I remembered how he had wanted a quick, surgical separation, after which I was to take my polluting presence away from them all, preferably to France. How could I have gone away to a place where there was no hope of glimpsing the dear faces of my children?

That was all in the past. I would not hold it against him now. Grief sliced through my heart and this time the pain was for him. Poor Charles! Gone so early from this earthly life! I remembered him full of vigour, with a love for the whimsical and the absurd. How he made us laugh with his antics and his theatricals!

I wished to see him one last time. I wanted to be there, a part of the magic circle of our family, consoling one another, instead of weeping bitter tears alone, forever an outcast.

Grief brings a family together. Should I go to Gad's Hill? My children would be devastated by their loss. They had a deep and abiding love for him. He was everything to them. They would be hurting badly.

But I knew I would not go. I did not have the courage. Moreover, the children would turn to their Aunt Georgy, the mother they have been taught to love. Whom was I deluding? The children did not need me. Nobody needed me.

A great melancholy settled over me but the tears did

not come for a long time. When they came, I tried to check them back. I had no right to weep over him. No, I had every right; he was the father of my children and that was one connection no one could deny. The dam broke and I sobbed into my pillow for a long, long time.

I wished I could see Charles and bid him goodbye. I was filled with sorrow for his death and remorse for his life, and I wanted to absolve him of all his sins against me, his wife he had vowed to love and to cherish. God knows he needed my forgiveness.

I did something I had vowed never to do again. I took out his letters and read them, and tried to feel the love he once had for me. Where had that love gone? Why had it been replaced by such a deep hatred that when our son died, alone and forlorn in faraway India, he did not share one single word of sorrow with me. He was our son, created out of our bodies. Did he not deserve our joint blessings? Could we not come together in our sorrow? That was when I had vowed never to think of him again with any tender feelings, I knew then without a vestige of doubt that he was a monster and as villainous a creature in any of his books!

And now that he was cold and dead, the hatred seeped out of my heart. I read his letters written during our courtship and shed tears over them. What children we had been then and so happy too.

As news about Charles' death spread, a string of callers arrived. They came to offer their condolences, and like it was after my separation, they also came out of avid curiosity. They murmured their condolences and I answered them civilly. They thought I did not notice but I saw them shoot quick glances at my face. They were kind but could not help being curious. They wanted to ascertain whether I had shed tears. They wanted an answer to the riddle that had puzzled them for the last twelve years: did I care for Charles?

Before the callers came, I bathed my eyes and face with cold water and composed my 'public face'. I was undecided about my clothing. What should it be? Mourning or not? My indecision rose not from my heart but from the fact that Charles did not wish me to be his wife. My gown was anyway dull so I added a black shawl and left it at that.

The funeral was to be held on the fourteenth, I learnt, and tried to carry on through the days as if the body of my husband did not lie in the same city. Helen knew I suffered. She was the one with whom I let down my guard and sometimes sobbed in her arms. It was strange that my grief came in such violent fits.

What is it about death that wipes clean the slate of bad memories? I did not remember my husband's harshness, my memories were only of the love and tenderness we had shared. As the day of the funeral approached, I grew determined to be present. What harm would my presence do? But Charley was given the unenviable task of telling me I should not go; Georgy felt Charles would not have wanted it.

The papers reported that the grave would be left open for three days, for mourners to pay their respects. The burial site was flooded with people who filed past the grave and offered flowers. Helen understood, and was by my side at Charles's grave, before we were jostled and pushed aside by the multitude come to pay their respects.

*** ***

Charley had a copy of his father's will. He did not want me to read it. "You will not like it," he said.

"I haven't liked many things these past years and I've had no choice but to live with them. Your father did all possible harm to me when he was alive, what more can he do? The will may provide the last nail in the coffin of my marriage."

I knew Charles would not leave me anything, actually, all I wanted him to leave me was an apology. I did not get it. Instead, my cruel, stubborn husband had reached out from the grave and delivered one final blow. When I finished reading the will, I could not restrain my tears.

Charley took the paper away. "I did not want you to read it. You are upset about the bequest to Ellen Lawless Ternan, but it is expected. I'm surprised it is not larger."

I give the sum of £1,000 free of legacy duty to Miss Ellen Lawless Ternan, late of Houghton Place, Ampthill Square, in the county of Middlesex.

"No Charley, that hurt has subsided. It is an old man's folly with a young girl. What wounds me is that even in

165

death he has sought to drive my children away from me. Did he not do enough harm during his lifetime? He has added the solemnity of his own death so that my children should feel guilty of disregarding his wishes if they try to reconcile with me."

I solemnly enjoin my dear children always to remember how much they owe to the said Georgina Hogarth, and never to be wanting in a grateful and affectionate attachment to her, for they know well that she has been, through all the stages of their growth and progress, their ever useful self-denying and devoted friend.

And I desire here simply to record the fact that my wife, since our separation by consent, has been in the receipt from me of an annual income of £600, while all the great charges of a numerous and expensive family have devolved wholly upon myself.

Once again, he made me out to be the gainer in the separation. What was the mutual consent he harped upon? What choice had he given me? He was like a mad man, desperate to throw me away, at any cost! What was the 600 pounds compensation for? No amount of money would compensate for the ache I had felt to hold my baby in my arms. My last born, my darling Plorn was only six when I was cast away! Yet he had recorded for posterity that while I was comfortable in my annuity, he labored under family responsibility. He only had to take me back and tear away the agreement.

The will reopened old wounds, and once again I was in the labyrinth of unanswered questions. I never really had understood why our world crashed. We started out right. I loved Charles and I knew he loved me. I could not think it was all a pretence because he showed his preference for me in so many ways. No one was surprised when he asked me to marry him. Even before the wedding, he considered me his wife. He wanted me to come to his lodgings and prepare breakfast for him, he said he wanted to see me the first thing in the morning.

Charles was different in those early days. He listened to my opinions, he liked to hear me sing. He joined in our musical evenings and with his high spirits, enlivened our evenings. He found our family cultured and well bred. He was impressed by my education and my intellect.

Charles was passionate and loving. Our first child was born nine months after we were joined in wedlock.

He showed his love in many ways. Sometimes he was hard on me but that was his way with all of us. He would be very loving but would get annoyed over small transgressions like a disordered chair or picture. There were times when he wanted me with him for a social gathering, and I did not accompany him due to my delicate state, which annoyed him.

But these were not reasons enough for him to turn into a bitter foe. It was a riddle and he had gone to his grave with the answer.

NINETEEN

Georgina, Again

"Helen, I've been thinking about asking Georgina and Mamie to visit me," I said, a few months after Charles' demise.

"No, you are not inviting Georgina. How can you forget what she has done to you? If anything, she should come to see you and ask for your forgiveness."

"And when is that likely to happen? No, it is I who must make the first move."

"Why? She robbed you of everything. She is the guardian of your children, Charles left her all his effects and assets and eight thousand pounds. She must be crowing! Nowhere would a spinster have edged out her sister so completely."

"Helen, I said Georgina and Mamie. Kate now visits me frequently but Mamie hasn't come. I want to see her and this is the only way."

"All right. Send word through Charley and don't be

surprised if she doesn't come."

But Georgina came, and to my great relief, so did Mamie. Mamie was thirty- five and it was likely she would not marry. She had a pinched look about her face, and in a way, looked older than Georgy. Georgy was forty-three, the age I was when I had last seen her, twelve years ago.

I held out my arms to Mamie and as she hesitated. I stepped forward and embraced her. She held herself stiffly and looked at Georgy.

Georgy met me in a matter of fact way, as if we had recently parted. There was a bold look in her eye. She looked around the small room and said, "You've a nice place here. It's quite cozy."

Helen was in the room. She had insisted she would remain with me but would not speak to Georgy. Georgy dominated the conversation. She was very busy, she told us, organizing Charles' papers and answering letters of condolences, which kept pouring in. She was sensible to the honour he had done in placing his trust in her, by leaving his papers in her care.

Helen was glaring so hard at Georgy that I had to nudge her. The visit was not successful but I was satisfied. A start had been made. I repeated my invitation a week later and as frequently as possible. Georgy often sent her excuses but sometimes came, with or without Mamie.

Georgy, I found, had become an incessant talker, and

most of her conversation was about Charles, the children, and how much she had sacrificed for them.

"Why do you permit her to speak like that?" Helen asked me crossly.

"Don't worry, she does not upset me. I find her visits revealing. I watch her mouth, and her eyes, and the way she sends quick glances at me, and checks whether her darts have wounded me. She purses her mouth disapprovingly when she speaks of others, and preens when her anecdotes are about herself, Charles, or Ellen."

"Ellen Ternan, the mistress? Georgy speaks about her?"

"They were all good friends, she tells me. Charles brought her to Gad's Hill sometimes, the other visits were when he took Georgy and Mamie to Paris. Charles had settled Ellen in Paris, and they would all meet sometimes. Georgy praises Ellen and tells me she is very fond of her."

"This is beyond anything! How could Charles let that woman meet Mamie!"

"Georgy tells me he thought very highly of her. She was everything proper and dignified."

Helen could not stomach this. The next time Kate visited, she asked her, "Are you on friendly terms with Ellen Ternan? Georgy often speaks of her."

Kate shrugged. "I've met her, of course, but she's no friend of mine. Aunt Georgy made much of her, to get Papa's approval, and Mamie followed Aunt Georgy."

"What do you think of her?" Helen asked.

"She's nothing wonderful. She isn't very pretty but she has a sharp mind, and she's fond of reading."

"Is she kind," I asked, faltering, "do you think she loved your father?"

"Oh no, she didn't. She was with him to better herself and her family. She and her mother were intelligent enough to snare him, but I don't blame them. She was just eighteen, used to genteel poverty, and she had the most powerful and respected man in the country at her feet."

"She must have been attracted to those qualities," I said.

"No. He wanted to believe she was a pure, innocent, helpless heroine from his books, and she played the part. But she has a sharp mind and nerves of steel. I observed her, and saw the disgust and contempt in her eyes, when she thought herself unobserved. I overheard her converse sensibly with her mother but as soon as Papa joined them, she put on a sickeningly sweet act for him, and he fluttered around her, picking up her handkerchief and parasol. She did not love him; I rather think she hated him and her difficult position but he loved her."

The next time when Georgy simpered and started another anecdote about dear Nelly, I asked, "You did not think it was in bad taste for Charles to let his unmarried daughter mingle with his mistress?"

"You should not use that word. It was not like that at all. The bequest in the will might have given you the idea but if she was what you called her, he would have left her more. He left her a thousand pounds, the same as he left Mamie. She was like another daughter to him."

Georgy spoke fast, all the time looking me in the eye. She had learnt well.

"Georgy, after being forced out of my home, I've spent a lot of time thinking about Charles and his ways. You may deny it if you please but Charles left the thousand pounds only for that reason, so that anyone who suspected the connection would be put off the scent by the smallness of the bequest. That was his way. He would create a smokescreen of words and hide his meaning in them. His income from his American tour itself was in the nature of twenty thousand pounds at a conservative guess, or that is what the newspapers reported. Charles was always good with investments. I am certain he provided separately for her, either through you or by some other means."

Georgy flushed a guilty red. "What do you mean you were forced out? You left because you wanted to."

"Why would I suddenly want to leave my home?"

"Kate, you quarreled and you left. You never understood Charles."

A maid came in and I remained silent. After she left, Georgy said, "Nelly was not like the usual actress, which is why Charles wanted us to befriend her. She was quite unspoilt when Charles met her. There was nothing sordid in their relationship. She did not try to snare him or anything. Rather, he wooed her. He was quite in love with *her*."

This was the Georgina I knew, who would find ways and means to insert unkind darts.

"Georgina, what Charles did is not called wooing. There is a baser word for it. I agree Ellen was unspoilt. When Charles forced me to visit them, I guessed she did not have any idea of Charles' intentions. But Charles was not unspoilt. He set out to seduce her."

"No, he did not."

"What other word is there for it? She was young enough to be his daughter. He was plying her with gifts for herself and for her family. He helped her mother, sisters, and housed them all in a well-appointed house purchased by him. He was rich and powerful, she was poor and helpless. When she finally gave herself to him, it was a shameful thing. She must have loathed herself and him too, that is, if she was as principled as you tell me she was."

"God, how you hate him!"

"Judge for yourself. Suppose, when Kate was eighteen, a rich and powerful man of forty-five, married and the father of ten children, whose wife was alive, pursued Kate for two years, during which she lost her reputation, and made her his mistress, what would you think of such a man? Would his behavior be called wooing or slaking his sinful lust?"

"I don't want to listen to this."

"Listen this once and never again. Charles broke the laws of church, society, and of decent behavior. If it was mutual passion, if he had fallen in love with someone who loved him in return, and they were both unable to live without each other, if we had been miserable in our marriage and had not been able to live together, then I would have understood. But Charles broke up our family to seduce a girl younger than his two children, and forced a separation on me, that I've not been able to forgive."

"He was unhappy. Both of you were unhappy and miserable."

"You are repeating what he put out to the world. You know we were happy and content."

"Yes, but sometimes he was annoyed and irritable."

"Didn't our parents ever snap at each other? Didn't our father say that Mama nagged him, did not Mama say he spent more time with his work than with her? Charles and I were happy. We did not have many quarrels because I often gave in."

"Charles did not like that."

"No. What he did not like was that I *always* did not give in, and I criticized him. He was changing and he did not know it. The change was not a good one."

"What do you mean?"

"When I first met Charles, he was idealistic. From his earliest days, he plunged into social causes. He had a clear picture about what was morally right or wrong. He did not care for society's opinion but used his own judgment. He was an idealistic man, who wanted to uplift women whom society had discarded. I remember the glow on his face when he kept me awake late into the night and described his plans for these women. They are not bad women, their circumstances are bad, he said. He wanted them to leave off being prostitutes, mistresses, and learn a skill, become literate, and start a life as wives and mothers.

"I do not know what happened along the way. Perhaps it was the great success he achieved, the great adulation, or the friends he made who took him into a world which had a different morality; some of them lived openly with their mistresses..."

"But Kate, your differences are of much before. Forster is writing Charles' biography, as you know. He showed me a letter from the early days of your marriage, where Charles said you were not suited."

"Early days?" I was surprised until I recollected something. "Georgy, please check the date of the letter. I am certain it will be sometime before or after childbirth. Charles was always grumpy and unhappy during those times, because..well, he was a young husband who liked the company of his wife."

"Forster showed me another letter. Charles again mentioned he was not happy in his marriage."

"When was this?"

"This was a few months before your separation."

"That must be after he met Ellen. Georgy, Forster was

Charles' close friend. He shared everything with him. Don't you think if Charles was unhappy and 'always miserable' as he published in the newspaper, he would have complained a little more in those twenty-two years? Our wedding anniversary and Forster's birthday fell on the same day and we celebrated it together. You were to be jealous, you wanted to be included, until Charles told you that the day was only for him and his dear Kate, remember?"

"That was in the beginning."

"Not very much in the beginning, I think. You were eighteen or nineteen, and were always seeking out Charles, and as he loved attention, he was starting to call you his little pet. We were already married for more than ten years. If we were ill- suited, we would not be spending so much time with each other."

"But you were not suited in later years."

"Georgy, when you were twenty-five, you received a proposal of marriage; Augustus Egg had proposed to you. You were fond of him and were sure he loved you. You declined the proposal, though I wanted you to reconsider. Why?"

"Because Charles thought he wasn't good enough for me."

"What did you think? That he wasn't as good as Charles? I was annoyed with Charles then, as was Mama. I felt he was ruining your life. You were of the right age to start a family of your own, not waste it where you were no longer needed."

Georgy started as if I had hit her.

"Georgy, please listen to me. I did not say *not wanted*, I said *not needed*. I loved you dearly then. You were my baby sister, whom I had helped bring up. You came to us after our return from America. Charley was six, Mamie five, Kate three, and poor Walter not yet two. We had maids and nurses to look after the children. I suggested your visit because I had missed my family during my stay in America. Charles agreed because he thought you would be a help to me."

"You accuse me of not helping out? After all that I did for you and your children?"

"Georgy, let us have some plain speaking this once. But if it will again turn us into enemies, I will stop this instant. However, it was you who opened the pandora's box with your talk about Ellen."

I waited, and when Georgy did not stop me, I continued.

"You were quite unlike Mary. In fact, you were more a child than a young woman and instead of helping me or giving me company, you were happy with the children. You played with them and eased the job of their nurses. I did not mind, you were just out of the schoolroom, and no more than a child yourself. I saw you more as a daughter than a sister. As the other children were born every year or two, you made a place for yourself. You became the 'voice' of Charles. Any order he gave, you were after the maids until they implemented it. You repeated whatever he said, and liked whatever he liked. You liked to think both of you were alike. You once told me I was weak- willed while you had a strong personality. The truth is you had totally subjugated your will and suppressed your personality. That was why, when Augustus wanted you to be his wife, you only thought what Charles thought. You did not consider your life."

"And I don't regret it. I spent the best part of my life for the children and Charles. You may not be grateful, but he was."

I knew I had already spoken too much. Georgy would not accept the truth. The servants had sometimes grumbled that she rode roughshod over them. She had developed a sharp tongue and a wit that hurt. She did not even spare me. By the time she was twenty-seven, she was sharp-faced and sharp- tongued, except when Charles was around. Then she would remind him of his engagements though he did not need a reminder, and point out some arrangement she had done exactly the way he wanted. She was not above causing trouble between us. She would not pass on a message, or artlessly repeat something about me or the children that Charles did not like.

I had wanted her to leave but did not know what to do. She was not an employee to be dismissed. She was my sister. Charley and Kate saw through her but not Mamie. Mamie had always wanted her father's approval. I think she saw Georgy as being in his good graces, and clung to her.

What was to become of Mamie?

Georgy did not visit again for many days. When she came next, it was after the sad demise of my son, Sydney, two years after his father's. He was coming to England from India, and was on sick leave. He died during the long voyage and was buried at sea. This was the second time death had snatched away a son of mine. Sydney was only twenty-five.

Georgy came, as did Mamie, and my other children. I was shattered and took to my bed.

Sydney had also got into debts during Charles' lifetime, and Charles had hardened his heart against him. I was hoping when Sydney returned, we would, as a family, help his turn a new leaf. I believed that my children had floundered because of the separation of their parents, and the knowledge that their father preferred Ellen over them. They would also have read their father's notice in the newspapers, and believed that their mother had never loved them.

A year after Sydney, Charles Collins passed away. He was suffering with cancer. Kate was widowed after thirteen years of marriage.

Kate was different from all my children. She was brave and loving and spirited, and had been her father's favorite. Yet, she was not blind to the injustice he had done, and carried the burden of guilt, both hers and her father's, I think.

She visited me more often than my other children and brightened up my day with her presence. But sometimes her brightness felt like a brittle mask that covered the arid years of her marriage.

A year after her husband died, she married Charles Edward Perugini. Like Kate, he was an artist and painted portraits. Perugini and she were well suited, with similar tastes, and they encouraged each other's talent. Kate also posed for him, and helped when he worked on a big canvas. They had a son but the child left for his heavenly abode when he was just seven months old. Kate bore her loss bravely and immersed herself in her painting, and derived satisfaction from the fact that her paintings were being exhibited in the Royal Academy.

Kate was looking happier in this marriage, yet I think she had stopped believing in love as a part of marriage when she was eighteen.

I continued to live in my house but was assured of a welcome by my children and of course, by dear Helen. I loved my grandchildren, and delighted in their love for me.

Yet I could not persuade myself that the long separation had not left our relations unmarked. For one, we did not speak about Charles, or the intervening years. I did not ask my children how they had fared, and whether they had missed me. I did not reassure them that I had always loved them because that would mean calling their father a liar.

I was grateful for the present, and hoped for a better future, that was all.

Mamie continued to hold herself aloof. I wanted her to come and live with me but she preferred to make her home with Georgy, and repeated the words from Charles' will that Georgy was her *self-denying and devoted friend*, and she could not leave her.

TWENTY

Recording for Posterity

G eorgy's visits had reduced considerably, and the conversations had become decidedly one-sided. She spoke and I listened.

One evening, when she visited me, Helen and Kate were present, and both of them were quite agitated, the reason being an article in the newspapers, published on the occasion of Charles' seventh death anniversary.

"Have you read this?" Helen flung the paper at Georgina.

Georgina glanced at the article and said, "Yes. I read it before it was published. The public is still interested in Charles, and this is the week of his death anniversary. The young man who wrote the article came to me for personal details, to help the public know their beloved writer a little better. I was worried he would write something foolish and tarnish Charles' memory. I asked him to show the article to me before sending it in."

Kate glared at her aunt, while Helen pounced on her. "How could you? Have you not done enough harm?"

"What's wrong with the article?"

"Have you read what he has written about Catherine? It is a hundred times worse than what Charles had accused her of. She is pictured as almost an imbecile, someone Charles put up with for twenty-one years due to the magnanimity of his nature. Every year the newspapers malign her more and more."

"It is our duty to protect Charles' reputation at any cost. Don't forget, he is called the Inimitable. I am sure Catherine understands. He was asking awkward questions about..well, I had to make him see that Charles had borne as much mental agony and physical hardship as could be expected of a Christian."

"At the cost of your sister?"

"Nobody knows what happened to Catherine after the separation; I daresay many people even think she is deceased. It is our duty to Charles to protect his name and guard his legacy."

While Helen and I stared at Georgy, Kate stood up. "I can't take it any longer. My father was a wicked, wicked man and what he made us do to our mother was evil. I find it intolerable that the world thinks of him as a genial human, all good cheer and kindness, and embodying the spirit of family Christmas. I will speak out, and let the world know him as what he was."

Kate rushed out, leaving Georgy to stare after her. "She's not in a condition to go alone," Helen said, and ran out after Kate.

"You have to stop Katey," Georgy told me, in a stricken voice. "She must not tell about Ellen. All will be lost, and after I've taken such pains to keep Ellen quiet."

"Ellen quiet? Do you meet her still?"

"I write to her, and Mamie does, too. She is our friend of course, and I don't want to lose sight of her. Only a few people knew about her, and while they are all loyal to Charles and will not besmirch his name, they may let slip a careless word, which could lead some newspaperman to contact her. The newspapers in America would pay a big amount for Ellen's story."

"Where is she now? Do you support her still?"

"She has been clever. She started out again and declared herself fourteen years younger, she always looked less than her years, and married a much younger man. Her husband does not know of the deception. She is secure from publicity in her new married name of Mrs. Robinson but she has a temper. I don't know what she will do if she feels slighted. That is why I've told Mamie we should continue with our attentions. Please explain to Kate why she must be silent. If she starts something, we don't know where it will end."

"Kate will not say anything. I know her. Neither will the others. It is now seven years. Forster has come out with Charles' biography, as have some other friends. They have loyally preserved Charles' image, and blamed me."

Georgina ignored my pained words, or did not notice them at all. She wrung her hand and said, "Catherine, you don't know how I worry! There is so much you don't know! If only you knew what a burden I carry! Where Ellen is concerned, we are forever obliged to her."

"Why?"

Georgy looked uncomfortable. "You may not know but a malicious rumour started after Charles died. Some people whispered Charles had gone to see Ellen the day before he expired. He collapsed in her house, at Peckham, and Ellen brought him to Gad's Hill, with the help of trusted people."

"I thought very few people knew about Ellen, and where she lived. How can there be rumours?"

"No..yes, is it not strange? If someone gets to Ellen and she confirms the story, ...the rumour, imagine the scandal! All will be lost."

Georgy looked uncomfortable and with sudden insight, I guessed at the truth. Charles had been stricken down at Ellen's, and Georgy was scared she would tell.

"They were using false identities, were they not?" I asked.

"Yes. The house was rented to Charles Tringham, Ellen was Mrs. Tringham," Georgy replied, not immediately realizing the purport of her words.

"How convenient."

"You should not judge, you do not know her. Ellen could have exploited Charles and her association with him but she has remained silent. You were right in your guess that Charles provided for her, in addition to the thousand pounds. Forster and I helped her in getting her inheritance, after which she went to France. She married only last year. The truth is I'm happy she has used a false age because now I have her secret, and she will not be able to ruin us, don't you see?"

I fixed a smile for Georgy, to show I understood but I did not. I only felt the pain of betrayal, which was surprising because I thought I had overcome my past.

"Catherine, do you have Charles' letters? Have you kept them? I suspect you may have destroyed them."

"Why do you want to know?"

"I've an idea and am working on it. You must know, Charles made a big bonfire when he sold Tavistock House and burnt all the letters he had received over the years. He requested his friends to destroy the letters he had written to them. Few did, but most disregarded his wishes. I kept his letters, though I told him I had burnt them."

"What is your idea?" I asked Georgy, as she smoothed her gown, and toyed with her gloves.

"It is to do with Mamie. She needs to take an active interest in something. I've started collecting Charles' letters from his friends and I want Mamie to compile them into a book, with a narrative for each year."

186

"Why would you want to include the letters he wrote to me? Will that not be a scandal?"

"Oh no! They will show him the family man he was, I think," said Georgy, looking me in the eye.

"I've kept the letters but they are personal. I would not want them to be published. Forster published Charles' letter in the biography. Does that not suffice?" I asked, suddenly angry. I was referring to the letter Charles had written to Forster after returning from Manchester.

This was the first of the letters he wrote to a few people, speaking about how ill suited we were.

Poor Catherine and I are not made for each other, and there is no help for it. It is not only that she makes me uneasy and unhappy, but that I make her so too -- and much more so. She is exactly what you know, in the way of being amiable and complying; but we are strangely ill-assorted for the bond there is between us. God knows she would have been a thousand times happier if she had married another kind of man, and that her avoidance of this destiny would have been at least equally good for us both. I am often cut to the heart by thinking what a pity it is, for her own sake, that I ever fell in her way; and if I were sick or disabled to-morrow, I know how sorry she would be, and how deeply grieved myself, to think how we had lost each other. But exactly the same incompatibility would arise, the moment I was well again; and nothing on earth could make her understand me, or suit us to each other.

Her temperament will not go with mine. It mattered not so much when we had only ourselves to consider, but reasons have been growing since which make it all but hopeless that we should even try to struggle on.
The fire I thought had died down, blazed again. How wickedly Charles had used his pen against me! In this letter, he said I was amiable but ill suited, a few months later he published I had a mental peculiarity and I did not care for the children. Soon after that he insisted I had wanted the separation and was glad to be rid of the children!

"Catherine, you can't want to keep the letters. What pleasure can they give you?" Georgy pressed.

"None at all, I'll be well rid of them," I said, and rushed into my room. I pulled out the trunk and threw the letters on the bed. Georgina, who had followed me, quickly gathered them. She did not care to see I had tears in my eyes. The old wound just would not heal.

The next morning, the maid found one packet of letters lying under the bed. Georgina had missed it. The letters were tied with a silk ribbon, in a love knot; they were the ones Charles had written during the months before our marriage.

Helen was annoyed with me. "Why did you give her the letters? She will find a way to use them against you."

"What more harm can she do? Does it matter? Didn't she say she has to paint me darker every year so that no one suspects about Ellen? You can expect next year's articles to describe how Charles had to keep me locked up sometimes, for my own good, naturally."

Kate was also not pleased I had given the letters. But when I learnt Mamie was indeed working on them, I was happy.

TWENTY-ONE

Finding Answers

I know I am dying. Helen tried to hide it from me, but Georgy told me I've cancer. Even otherwise, I would have known.

I do not mind the dying, but I wish the pain was not so severe. The frequent dosage of laudanum is of little help.

Kate comes often, as do Mamie and Georgy. Helen hovers, masking her feelings under a brisk demeanor. Her daughter, May, is a delight. I love her dearly.

Plorn is in Australia, and writes regularly. I treasure his letters. Charley continues in his faithful ways. His family has grown considerably; he also has money troubles.

When the pain is very intense, it opens a window in my mind and old memories tumble out. I see my younger self, flushed and laughing, with my lover, sometimes in the garden of my father's house, sometimes on the ship to America, and sometimes at Gad's Hill.

I've taken to reading Charles' letters. I only have the letters he wrote during our courtship, but they are a delight. How sweetly he had loved me!

I wish I had kept all my letters, and not given them to Georgina. I find I can ignore my pain when I read the letters.

Kate frequently complains that Georgy is using my letters to her advantage. She has inked over and even cut out many parts, and does not intend to include many of the later letters. She wants to show that Charles and I had drifted apart a few years before we separated. She was, however, including all the letters Charles wrote to her.

Charles had started writing to Georgy a few years after she came to live with us. She had demanded 'her' letters, and Charles had indulged her. He had included a letter for her along with my letter, and had continued the practice. He had never written to her alone, until that fateful trip to Manchester.

"I've seen the draft of the compiled letters," Kate said, "and most of your letters are missing. When I asked Aunt Georgy, she said she had the best interests of all of us. Mama, I think you should take back your letters."

I know Kate is right. Every year, articles about Charles, and the biographies that came out, project me in a worse light. I am the helpmeet gone bad, a pitiable cross Charles had to bear.

Kate, so like her father in many ways, has also become his most critical child. She will not condone his actions, and wants to undo the wrongs he had done. Georgy does not understand, and neither do I, when she insists that the public that worships him has a right to know him, flaws and all. She is sickened by his public persona.

Until now we seldom spoke about Charles because it was too painful, but now, with me dying, Kate asked, "Why did he do this to you? Why did he change into a monster?"

"Kate, it is all over and done with. You love him, I know."

"But all those lies! Mama, I was not a little girl when you left. I was nineteen and remembered how we had lived until then. We had good times, and you loved us. But he forced you out of our home for that .. that .. woman. He never cared for you or for us. The younger boys, when they came home, were scared he would send them away also if they displeased him. After you left, we were all insecure, and had no one to turn to. Until then, he was the greatest person I knew. I was proud to be his daughter but after he maligned you and kept us away from you, I hated him."

"But you loved him, too," I said, patting Kate, as she angrily wiped away her tears.

"It wasn't even as if there was anything special about Ellen. She was young and pretty, and intelligent, but she was as old as me. It was disgusting the way he pursued her. How did he change so much?"

"Is that not how it often is? You are a woman of the

world now. Don't men prefer young and shapely women to middle-aged fat wives? And I was fat."

"Do all husbands break up their families if their wives turn stout?" Kate demanded.

Kate looked so like the 'Lucifer Box' of her childhood that I couldn't help smiling.

"That was not his only reason."

"He had a reason?"

"I understand his reasons now. Your father was an artist. He was practical in many ways, yet a dreamer in some ways. He may have dreamt of a romance that would sweep him away. His first love was Maria Beadnell; for him it was love, for her a flirtation. He loved me next and I returned his love in full measure. But we became husband and wife, and soon had to deal with many mundane things. It was love, but not a grand passion. Maybe your father felt cheated, and as he grew older, he thought there was no possibility of his dream romance. He grew restless and had spells of unhappiness, especially after he finished a book and did not have anything to occupy him. Very likely, he saw me as the reason of his unhappiness. He thought, perhaps, if he had not married me he would have found someone else and lived his dream. Like I said, he was not practical in this area. Whomever else he would have married would most probably have been tied down with childbirth and childrearing, the same as I was.

"When he saw Ellen, he made her the embodiment of his great romance. What he felt for her was probably lust but he saw it as the love of his life. He pursued her. He had an active conscience which made him find reasons for his behavior. He had been miserable, he told himself, and soon told the rest of the world. Another man would have taken the woman as his mistress and not broken up his family and scattered his children. But Charles was living a romance and though he made Ellen his mistress, he told himself she was pure and noble and unsullied.

"If he did not blame me, it meant he was like Mr. Quilp pursuing Littte Nell. So he rewrote the story of our lives, the way he rewrote an episode of his novels when he did not like it. And he believed what he wrote. He mesmerized himself, don't you see? He wrote himself the hero's part and consigned me as the villain. That was the only way he could proceed with his romance.

"One more thing. He assigned Ellen the part of the heroine, and as he was fond of attributing tragic circumstances, and innocence and helplessness to his heroines, so he did with Ellen. Georgy has told me a lot about Ellen, as have you. Ellen was quite unlike the heroines of his books. She was strong and intelligent, with a mind of her own. Yet he saw her as all sweetness, goodness, and innocence."

"You mean to say, whatever happened was only because he wanted something not attainable, and imagined that he had found it at last?" Kate asked, looking doubtful.

"Yes. Bring me Forster's book and I will prove my point."

Kate got the book and I opened it to show her a passage I had marked. Forster was Charles' closest friend, he was loyal to him and stood by him, yet he had given an insight into Charles' character that explained his actions.

He (Charles) had otherwise, underneath his exterior of a singular precision, method, and strictly orderly arrangement in all things, and notwithstanding a temperament to which home and home interests were really a necessity, something in common with those eager, impetuous, somewhat overbearing natures, that rush at existence without heeding the cost of it, and are not more ready to accept and make the most of its enjoyments than to be easily and quickly overthrown by its burdens.

"That is precisely what happened to your father. After twenty-two years of working on his books, and his social causes, and the responsibilities of home and hearth which constituted of ten children and a wife, he rushed into an existence which he thought would give him unfettered enjoyment."

"And made you the scapegoat," Kate said, bitterly.

"To start with, knowingly, and later, as I explained, by convincing himself that he could not be so base, it had to be compelling circumstances that made him do it. Once he got hold of an idea, he did not let it go. I remember he had once written to me that *'the intense pursuit of any idea that takes complete possession of me, is one of the qualities that makes me different – sometimes for good; sometimes I dare say for evil – from other men'*.

"Do you mean to say he did not love Ellen?"

"I mean he did not hate me as much as he supposed he did and he did not love Ellen as much as he thought he did. He was stubborn and had to be always right. On our separation, he made two announcements to the world. Having made those statements about our marriage, he would not admit even to himself he was wrong. He would convince himself that his was a grand passion, a great romance, a fairy tale in which Ellen was the princess and he was fighting dragons for her.

"Foolish man. We had so much and the coming years could have been so fruitful. He would have continued the friendships he had forged and done a great good with his philanthropic works. You, Mamie, and the boys would have had a proper home. He would have lived peacefully, instead of rushing about living in different places and assuming false identities. We would have grown old together. He would have lived longer, I'm sure, he was strong and healthy and took a lot of exercise."

"How do you understand so much about him?"

"He was twenty-two when I met him. In many ways, we grew up together. I think I understood him the most. Yet, understanding our separation did not come easily. I blamed myself for many years, and believed the falsehoods he hurled at me. Later, I started observing other husbands and wives; I peeped as much as was possible into their lives, and I found Charles and I had lived the same, or even a better life. Ours had been a normal marriage and it should have lasted."

The long conversation tired me out but I hoped it brought Kate some comfort.

TWENTY-TWO

Outside the Magic Circle

Within a month it was Kate's turn to comfort me. The cancer had spread fast and I was painfully moving towards death.

The pain was so severe that it snapped the control of a lifetime. It broke my resolve never to speak about the ills I had suffered at the hands of Charles.

I told Kate about the times Charles had been cruel, and even deceitful. I shared the pain, the humiliation of his actions, starting with his obsession for Mary.

Kate, dutiful daughter that she was, tried to ease my bitterness with what were probably untruths. Charles had enquired about me many times, she insisted, and two days before he died, he had spoken to her about me and regretted that he had not been a better man. I listened to her, and tried to hold on to her words for strength, though they were as weak as straws.

As I drifted between a drugged sleep and coherent thought, I remembered Georgina's words. "Charles called Ellen his Magic Circle of One," she informed, her voice sweet with spite, "she was all he needed."

The Magic Circle. Charles always had a magic circle, or even circles, around him. He made friends easily and lavished his love on them. They also returned his affection in full measure and surrounded him, listening to his ideas, his views. Forster was a part of the Magic Circle, as was Wilkie Collins, Macready, and a horde of others, and Georgina. He read aloud to them, often enacting whole parts. There was a glow to these gatherings, he was like a bright star, and palpable on everyone's face was the pride and joy they felt in basking in his light.

Was I ever a part of his Magic Circle? Perhaps during our courtship when he played the besotted lover? Not even then because he shared more of his love rather than his thoughts with me. He wrote letters and even read out his plays but it was not because my opinion mattered; I was to him sweet Kate, who loved him and who listened to him. I was the convenient wife who performed her wifely duties and bore his children, who listened to him night after night but was not to give her opinion, and the one who was dispensable. I had always been outside the Magic Circle.

For me the magic circle was my husband and children around our hearth, the way he wrote in his stories. I liked to think it was the pleasantness of our home that he brought in his writings, and in his Christmas stories.

I was content to be a part of this circle. I did not crave any other. He could shine like a brilliant orb everywhere but I loved it that he found joy in our children and home.

He had pushed me out of this circle and saw to it that I remained outside. Everyone was made to close ranks against me but his viciousness destroyed the magic, too. Instead of a circle, my family degenerated into a huddle of frightened, unhappy, lonely souls, engulfing me in the sum total of their pain.

"What are you saying?" I hear Helen ask; I must have spoken my thoughts aloud.

Helen is by my bed. I try to speak but my mouth is dry. As usual, Helen understands, and spoons some water into my parched mouth.

"Why did you not have the broth? I've got some warm soup now. Come, have a little," Helen urges me, and succeeds where the maid and Kate have failed.

"Don't you know it's good for you?" she grumbles.

I smile. Twenty-one years ago, when my marriage dissolved, Helen had urged me to fight Charles, and used the same words when I refused.

"Don't you know what is good for you?" she had demanded and gone ahead to fight my battles and defy the great Charles Dickens.

Since then she has bullied me countless times with, 'What about you?', 'You owe it to yourself, Kate', and the more frequent 'Don't you know it's good for you?'

I realize I've always ignored Helen's well-meaning admonishments. She has tried to make me aware of a self within me, a self that is not mother, or wife, or even sister, but Kate, Catherine.

I realize I've allowed this self to be caricatured and lampooned, and become an object of scorn and pity. I've never come to the rescue of my own person. I've failed my own self.

My life is at an end now. Do I have time left to redeem a little of myself? I want to. Very much.

A week later, I ask Kate to retrieve a small packet from my table drawer.

"What is this, Mama?" she asks, giving me the packet.

I caress the small bundle, the letters with a silk ribbon tied in a love knot. I recognize them for what they are. They are the homage paid by a man to a young woman who was attractive, lively, talented, and who inspired love. They are an acknowledgement of her *worth*.

"Give these to the British Museum, that the world may know he loved me once," I tell Kate.

This   much   at   least   I   owe   myself.

About the Book

Like many people all over the world, I am an admirer of the works of Charles Dickens. I've spent long hours held captive by his stories, and by his characters; it seemed many of them were born not to tell the story but out of Dickens' love for them. They were funny, eccentric, with names one never came across in other books and they spoke in strange, quirky tongues. Yet, for all the multitude of people he created, and they were people in their own right, he mostly painted them black or white.

From the biographical notes appended to his books, I knew Charles Dickens grew up poor, and was sent to work in a factory at the tender age of twelve. Though he dropped out of school, he went on to become the foremost writer of the Victorian age. I learnt that he was married, had numerous offspring, with one son breathing his last in India. Because I live in India, I looked up the details of his son's last resting place.

Two years ago, I came across an article which mentioned that Dickens had separated from his wife because she was mentally weak and unfit for the role of wife and mother.

It was a matter of coincidence I read the article after starting on *Letters of Charles Dickens,* the three volume compilation of his letters to his family members, publishers, friends, and public, put together after his death by his daughter, Mamie Dickens and his sister-in-law, Georgina Hogarth.

I paid special attention to the letters addressed by him to his wife. They were addressed to his dearest Kate, his dearest love, his dearest Catherine. They continued until a year before the separation. They were long, chatty, affectionate letters, full of news and household enquiries. I therefore surmised that the affliction (which made her unfit to be his wife) was sudden, for the letters clearly showed him corresponding with a person of normal intellect and temper.

I thought a little less of Dickens; he had not stood by his wife in sickness, and had separated their children from her. On second thoughts, I wondered whether the article had underplayed Mrs. Dickens' problem. It must have been a dangerous form of mental disorder, forcing Charles Dickens to separate from his wife of twenty-one years. He always put families in the centre of his books and Christmas stories, he would not sever ties that bound Catherine to home and children without just cause, I decided.

The book, in its preface, mentioned that the compilation was meant to supplement the *Life of Charles Dickens* by his closest friend John Forster. I read the book but it left me confused. Forster did not dwell much on the separation. He hinted at Dickens being restless and for some years, unhappy in the married state, not for any fault of his wife but because of a feeling of incompatibility. He did not mention mental ailment in Dickens' wife.

A year later I read *Charles Dickens: A Life* by Claire Tomalin. The well researched book told an unbelievable, shocking truth. I read more books about Charles Dickens and the events surrounding his separation from Catherine, and also surfed the net.

Two images formed in my mind. Charles Dickens, creator of great fiction, a man of genius but ruthless, changeable, manipulative, selfish, hard. His allegations about his wife and his unhappy marriage were works of fiction, as successful and enduring as the rest of his works. Once again, he had used two colours: white for himself and black for Catherine.

The second image, and a very clear one, was of Catherine Dickens. I saw her clearly. I knew her. She was born a hundred and fifty years ahead of me, on the other side of the globe, in a repressive era, yet I've known, and seen women undergo much of what she experienced.

I knew her feelings and understood her silences. So I gave her a voice.

Acknowledgements

The book is based on facts, though (naturally) the conversations are fictional. The places, dates, and incidents are factual, and some dialogues include fragments from letters written by Charles Dickens and his friends.

The book is neither an attempt to add to the extensive facts that are already available about Charles Dickens nor to throw a new light on them. That work has been done by some very eminent people.

My short novel is my homage to the suffering of Catherine Dickens and to her strength.

Today, when women are much more independent, empowered with education and careers, no longer legally discriminated against, with virtually no social stigma attached to divorce, they still find it difficult to regain their lives after the collapse of a marriage.

Catherine Dickens was publicly dumped, maligned, removed from her home and separated from her children, the youngest being only six years old, for no fault of hers. Yet there is no evidence of her wallowing in self-pity, no angry outbursts against her husband. What is *recorded* is her dignified conduct and her continued efforts to reach out to her children and assure them of her love.

The facts about Charles and Catherine Dickens' lives, their marriage, etc., I've gleaned and corroborated from the following works, and I place here on record my debt of gratitude to the authors and also to the scholars whose work formed the basis of these books.

1. Georgina Hogarth and the Dickens Circle by A.A.Adrian
2. Charles Dickens: A Life by Claire Tomalin
3. The Letters of Charles Dickens edited by Mamie Dickens and Georgina Hogarth
4. Life of Charles Dickens by R.Sheldon Mackenzie
5. Dickens and Daughter by Gladys Storey
6. Dickens and Women by Micheal Slater
7. The Life of Charles Dickens by John Forster
8. The Other Dickens by Lilian Nayder
9. Charles Dickens: His Tragedy and Triumph by Edgar Johnson.

About the Author

Heera Dattta a.k.a Gita V. Reddy is a multi genre author who writes fiction for all ages. Her other notable book for adults is A Tapestry of Tears. In all, she has more than twenty published works. In addition to writing, she is also interested in art and has illustrated two picture books.

She lives in India with her husband and son.

For more details about Gita V. Reddy and her books, please visit her website www.gitavreddy.com.

A Tapestry of Tears

This is a collection of a novelette and twelve short stories. Woven into this tapestry are strands of love, loss, hope, and indomitable strength to face life.

Here is what Donna Foley Mabry, #1 bestselling author of Maude and other books has to say about the book. "Reddy writes in a straightforward prose that entices you to turn the page. For an American reader, it is truly a journey into another world."

From other amazon reviews:

"Gita Reddy is particularly perceptive about the dynamics of married relationships."

"To learn of another culture is amazing and this book will give you just that. Each story tells their story and the way that things are."

"The stories are like pages out of our own lives."

Excerpts

"But can you imagine what courage it takes to pour those two drops into the mouth of a babe? And the child you have carried yourself, one who is a part of your own body, whose heartbeat was a resonance of your own? Just as a man is not allowed to show fear on a hunt, women are not expected to waver in snuffing out that tiny life. Does a man remember the look in the eyes of a dying deer? Perhaps he does. A woman does not forget the face of the dead child. The child lives on as a phantom, clutching at her heart, and troubling her sleep. For the zamindar, the birth of a daughter is easily forgotten. He doesn't see the face because the child is completely wrapped up for the burial."

***

It was at Sherawal Kalan she realized why women the world over indulged themselves with needlework. For it was an indulgence, a soothing of the senses, a gentling of thoughts. They spoke, not in a rush, and not even to each other but their words were like a gentle brook, and took with them their hurts and worries. No man could understand the sisterhood of a sewing circle, Ramona thought, listening to them.

***

His silence never seemed to bother her. Like some ritual, she spent an hour sitting on the narrow chair and talking. She was like a shapeless sack of dull rancour. A thread of bitterness ran through all that she spoke about. She seemed to have a well of ill- feeling within her from which she drew out immeasurable cups of unfriendliness and acrimony. She didn't even seem to notice that she was always hostile.

There was no intelligence in her comments, no brilliant satire, no cutting sarcasm. She just sat there and spewed a mildly corrosive acid.

***

He felt her hand on his shoulder and shook his head to her gentle query. He was glad she couldn't see the tears that pricked his eyes. There was no reason for his behavior except that he felt very vulnerable and insecure, as if his home was a fragile nest built high above the ground and a single gust of wind would scatter it away.

Other Titles by the Author

King Neptune's Delite
Tara and the Giant Queen
Hunt for the Horseman
The Dinosaur Puzzle and Other Stories
Rangeela Tales (Book 1, Book 2, Book 3)
Rangeela Tales Complete Collection
Theft at the Fair and Other Stories
The Unicycle and Other Stories
Dearie : A Tale of Courage
The Forbidden Forest
The Magician's Turban
The Missing Girl
Krishta, Daughter of Martev
Make a Wish
Knife and fork
The Homeless Birds
Daksha the Medicine Girl

Picture Books for Ages 3-6

Super-Duper Monty

Hop and Chomp: A Caterpillar Story

Which is p and Which is q?

The Ant Thief

Bee-not-so-busy

Bala-Gala the Brave and Dangerous

The Alphabet Game –Interactive ABC book.